SYDNEY'S SCENE

Scandals and secrets have racked the Blackstone dynasty for decades, starting with their longtime feud with the Hammonds, and continuing with the oft-times off-color shenanigans of the Blackstone brood. But nothing the privileged clan has done rivals the latest news from the Australian "royal family." None other than shark-like corporate raider Jake Vance has been seen taking up space in the company's Pitt Street offices. What's a street-smart, self-made billionaire doing among the hallowed halls of old money?

Takeover rumors are not the only ones on the street. Australia's hottest "bad boy" has been seen over the

years with gorgeous models and millionaire heiresses. But now he's been spotted with his secretary, a small-town innocent named Holly McLeod. Someone ought to tell Ms. McLeod—and the Blackstones, for that matter—what many a woman already knows: Jake Vance may kiss like an angel, but getting involved with him is like making a deal with the devil. Then again, no devil has ever looked as good as Jake Vance....

Dear Reader,

I'm very excited about this, my second book. It germinated back in 2006 while I was still floating on my First Sale high. My favorite kiwi, Yvonne Lindsay, e-mailed me to ask if I'd like to join an author-led Down Under continuity. "You can say no if you want to," she added. Of course, I couldn't pass up the opportunity to work with a bunch of my favorite writers! Since then we've burned up the internet waves, with e-mails flying back and forth over the Pacific, brainstorming, plot-storming, character-storming, making sure our themes didn't clash, ensuring the timelines and backstory meshed. What a job!

I was particularly thrilled everyone loved my idea for the missing heir, and the mystery of the missing Blackstone baby is accompanied by a favorite theme of mine—office romance. There's something extremely forbidden about the whole scenario, don't you think? Throw into that the politics, sexual tension and inevitable gossip, and you have the makings of a potential disaster.

Again, I've set the story in a place familiar to me, the heart of Sydney's central business district, where I worked for many years. You may even recognize some places! The one artistic license I did take was removing the Sydney Hilton on George Street to make way for the Blackstone's Head Office. Ahh, the things we can do with fiction! If you want to read more about this book and the DIAMONDS DOWN UNDER series, go to www.diamonds-downunder.com. And as always, I'd love to hear from you at www.paularoe.com.

Love, Paula

PAULA ROE

BOARDROOMS
&
A BILLIONAIRE
HEIR

Published by Silhouette Books
America's Publisher of Contemporary Romance

A big hug and smoochy kiss to the Down Under Desireables for your support, hand-holding and encouragement: Bron, Tessa, Maxine, Yvonne and Jan. To Linley, my personal GMC wizard and finder-of-weak-spots. To MJ, who gave me such insightful suggestions and made my writing that much better. And my deep thanks to Andrew Burden of Canberra's Aviation Search and Rescue Centre who let me pick his brains about plane crashes and rescues in order to get everything *just right*.

SILHOUETTE BOOKS

ISBN-13: 978-0-373-76867-7
ISBN-10: 0-373-76867-2

BOARDROOMS & A BILLIONAIRE HEIR

Books by Paula Roe

Silhouette Desire

Forgotten Marriage #1824
Boardrooms & a Billionaire Heir #1867

PAULA ROE

Despite wanting to be a vet, choreographer, hairdresser, card shark and an interior designer (though not all at once!) Paula ended up as a personal assistant, office manager, aerobics instructor and software trainer for thirteen years (which also funded her extensive travel through the U.S. and Europe). Today she still retains a deep love of filing systems, stationery and traveling, although the latter is only in her dreams these days.

Paula lives near western Sydney's glorious Blue Mountains with her family, an ancient black cat and a garden full of rainbow lorikeets, magpies and willy wagtails. You can visit her at www.paularoe.com.

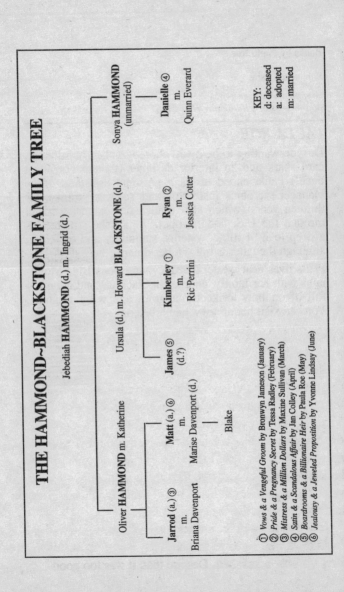

THE HAMMOND~BLACKSTONE FAMILY TREE

Jebediah **HAMMOND** (d.) m. Ingrid (d.)

Oliver **HAMMOND** m. Katherine

Ursula (d.) m. Howard **BLACKSTONE** (d.)

Sonya **HAMMOND** (unmarried)

Jarrod (a.) ③
m.
Briana Davenport

Matt (a.) ⑥
m.
Marise Davenport (d.)

James ⑤
(d.?)

Kimberley ①
m.
Ric Perrini

Ryan ②
m.
Jessica Cotter

Danielle ④
m.
Quinn Everard

Blake

① *Vows & a Vengeful Groom* by Bronwyn Jameson (January)
② *Pride & a Pregnancy Secret* by Tessa Radley (February)
③ *Mistress & a Million Dollars* by Maxine Sullivan (March)
④ *Satin & a Scandalous Affair* by Jan Colley (April)
⑤ *Boardrooms & a Billionaire Heir* by Paula Roe (May)
⑥ *Jealousy & a Jeweled Proposition* by Yvonne Lindsay (June)

KEY:
d: deceased
a: adopted
m: married

One

Wealth and power hung in the expansive boardroom, permeating every cherrywood panel, every thread of the tightly woven carpet underfoot.

The huge panoramic windows played right into that powerful aura, offering an unobstructed view of Sydney's CBD to the right, the curved dome of the historical Queen Victoria Building to the left. Subtle track lights highlighted the boardroom table where one woman and three men were rising to their feet. Jake Vance recognised each in turn: Kimberley Perrini; her husband, Ric, and current CEO of Blackstone Diamonds; Ryan Blackstone, Chief Financial Officer; and Garth Buick, the company secretary.

Jake had stood in the same spot days ago.

At that time, the room had been tense with stunned denial after his little bombshell. Despite that, it was too good a coincidence for Kimberley to pass up; he'd seen the burning curiosity in her shaken expression. Now, judging by the shell-shocked looks, they obviously had their proof.

Finding out your previously dead brother was very much alive was a life-changing event, even if that bit of gossip had been press fodder for months. But when that brother stood to gain a substantial chunk of the Blackstone fortune...

He swallowed bitterly. This wasn't in his ten-year plan. Making his first million, breaking into the U.S. market, giving back to his mother's favourite causes, yes. Even, eventually, a wife and kids. But not this. Not becoming Australia's walking, talking answer to the freakin' Lindbergh baby.

"James...Jake?" Kimberley Perrini said tentatively, obviously confused about how to proceed. He gave a curt nod and remained silent as she settled for sitting at the table. He noticed her crisp business suit, the efficient pulled-back hair, the air of sophistication and privilege radiating out as if she'd been born into it.

He shoved the uncharacteristic bitterness away and instead focused on his game plan—detecting weakness.

It was awkward, this first face-to-face meeting with his sister. *His sister, for God's sake.* He ignored the deeper implication and completed his study. The similarities between Kimberley and Ryan were obvious: dark hair with that widow's peak, green eyes. But where hers held optimistic caution, Ryan Blackstone's were full of outright hostility. It was in every smell that infused the ostentatious room, every movement and gesture the man made in his thousand-dollar suit.

Jake glanced over the table to where Garth Buick sat. The

two younger men, Ric and Ryan, were on their feet behind him, as if standing gave them a psychological advantage.

Jake had used that tactic many times before.

"We had April Kellerman's documents analysed, as well as those DNA tests," Ric Perrini said now, indicating Jake should take a seat.

"And?" Jake sat and Ric and Ryan followed suit.

"It appears that you are James Hammond Blackstone."

As one, they released a collective breath and the expectant hush in the room fanned out, spreading like a blanketing drift of snow. The air was just as chilly, with most of the freeze coming from the two men who had battled for the CEO's position after Howard's death.

Jake steeled his features to betray nothing. Emotion meant vulnerability, which meant your enemies had a weakness they could exploit. Show nothing, reveal nothing.

"So Howard was right all along," Kimberley finally said.

Ric shrugged. "Looks like it."

She frowned and opened her mouth to say something, but Ryan interrupted.

"We asked you here to discuss a few things. One, your plans for Blackstone's." Ryan's even tone belied the storm in his eyes. "And we'd like to make an offer for your shares."

Jake stifled his surprise. Interesting. Business first. "I'm not selling."

"You haven't heard our bid."

"I don't need to."

"Listen, Vance. If this is about payback or revenge—"

"Why would it?" Jake raised one eyebrow.

The men glanced at each other, regrouping. Finally Kimberley said slowly, "See it from our side. You and Quinn

Everard are close. There's been a long history of animosity between him and Howard—"

Jake smiled, an action he knew would throw them off balance. "Not my problem. I'm sure you've had me researched. So you know I never let personal feelings stand in the way of a business decision."

"What about Jaxon Financial?" Ric asked.

Jake paused, letting the barb sink in without showing it'd hit a sore spot. "That was over eight years ago. And it wasn't my company."

"But you were accused of insider trading," Ryan probed, his astute eyes unwavering.

Jake eased back in the leather chair and stretched his legs out, a calculated show of nonchalance. "Accused. Not charged."

"You lost millions. The CEO fired you."

"And I returned the favour eighteen months later when I bought them out. Look, we can go over my chequered history for hours, but it doesn't change the facts. The way I see it, you have two choices. Fight me for the claim, which would tie us up in court for years, and see the shares plummet. Or work with me on this. Blackstone's has a problem. Besides the press leak you've failed to plug, the company has been floundering since Howard's death. Share prices are dropping. The power struggle between you—" he nodded at Ric "—and you," then Ryan, "is unsettling the board, not to mention your shareholders. They're getting antsy."

"How do you know that?" demanded Ryan.

"I make it my business to know." Before Ryan could interject, Jake held up a hand. "I plan to fix that."

"Why?" Ryan asked, his eyes narrowed.

"Because I can."

"I meant—"

"I know what you meant. Like it or not, Howard made me a beneficiary. You're worried about Blackstone's collapsing? I can fix it. It isn't personal. It's business."

"So this is all just business to you?" Kimberley asked softly.

"Well, it's certainly not about family bonding."

He didn't miss her brief flash of dismay as her eyes met Ric's briefly.

"So what's your plan?" Ric said smoothly.

Jake sized him up. Ric Perrini looked hard, with a reputation to match. He'd been Howard's surrogate son, the only one deemed worthy to take over Blackstone's. The man probably felt threatened. Hell, they all did.

Hardly surprising. Jake traded on his unpredictable reputation; it sent fear and respect into the hearts of his adversaries and made them careless.

That's how he won.

He looked back to Kimberley, who'd been staring at him in silence. When he met her sharp green eyes, she refused to look away.

"You're the spitting image of Howard," she said now.

Thrown by such a personal comment, Jake frowned. He wasn't sure she meant that in a good way, either. Should he thank her? Ignore it? He opted for the simplest approach.

"Blackstone genes."

Kim hesitated. "You know we all thought Howard was out of his tree about you," she finally said. "I just can't believe you're actually alive."

He lifted his eyebrows and gave her a small, wry smile. "In the flesh."

Kim paused, a moment too long.

"You have something to say," Jake said calmly. "Just go ahead and say it."

"Don't you have questions about the family?" she asked curiously. "About Howard? Sonya? Vince?"

"Not particularly. I have a very efficient research department."

"So where have you been for the last thirty years?" Ryan asked tightly.

"Queensland first. Then when I was about ten, South Australia."

"And?" Kim prompted. Jake let them dangle for a few seconds before conceding, "I was kidnapped by Howard's housekeeper and her boyfriend. Two months after the ransom note, around midnight, their car crashed into the Lindon River, five kilometres north of—"

"Newcastle, yes, we've read the police report," Ryan interrupted. "Everyone assumed you'd drowned in the crash and floated out to sea."

"April Kellerman was driving by when the car crashed. She pulled me free."

"And kept you."

The scorn in Ryan's voice sent a fierce surge of protectiveness straight to Jake's chest. "Don't judge what you don't know," he warned softly, piercing the younger man with a steely look.

Silence abruptly fell.

"We need to know more if we're to prepare a press release," Kim finally said, then paused as a shadow passed over his features. "You don't trust us."

"I don't trust anyone."

"That's a nice attitude to have," Ryan muttered.

Jake raised one eyebrow. "I'm not the one with the press leak."

Ryan tensed as Perrini said, "You know the press will fill in the blanks with whatever they can find, true or not."

"I know."

Despite a thorough going over, Jake was determined not to give anything away under everyone's searching eyes. Kim's small sigh a few seconds later was the only indication he'd won. *Won what?* The victory came with a surprisingly bitter taste.

"Your birthdate is wrong," Kim said finally.

"Excuse me?"

"James was born on the fourth of August, 1974, which makes you thirty-four this year. Your official bio—as Jake Vance—had you celebrating your thirty-fifth birthday on the first of September."

He knew that they were just numbers on a bit of paper. That it didn't mean squat. Despite his cold logic, a small lick of helplessness bloomed in the pit of his belly. In a nanosecond, cold anger flooded in to douse it.

Anger that was unjustified. Anger that actually shamed him. Blaming a dead woman would solve nothing.

Outwardly he shrugged. "So I'm a Leo instead of a Virgo."

Ryan's snort of dark amusement echoed in the quiet room, one that twitched Jake's mouth in all-too-brief humour.

Then Garth rose and withdrew a piece of paper from a folder. "As Howard's first born, you are now the recipient of a considerable amount of wealth." The man handed the paper to Jake. "You know about the third of Howard's shares— fifty-one percent divided equally between you, Ric and Ryan. You also own Howard's Vaucluse mansion, Miramare, although Sonya Hammond was given the right to reside there for the rest of her life. The remainder of Howard's assets—personal investments, artworks, cash—are now divided between yourself and Ryan."

Jake studied the details in silence, pausing only to chance a glance at Kimberley. Even Howard's rumored lover, Marise Davenport-Hammond, had come away with a seven-figure sum, yet for his eldest daughter, the wife of his surrogate son Ric Perrini, nothing. Worse, he'd publicly and privately humiliated her with the gifting of his Bondi beach house to Ryan, a house where her mother had drowned.

He had to hand it to Kimberley—she met his scrutiny head on, the cool green gaze a study in calm.

Garth continued. "There's also an article that stipulates three Blackstones must sit on the board—at the moment it's Kimberley, Ryan and Vincent Blackstone, Howard's brother."

"I'm not after a board position."

"We're not giving you one. Yet," Ric said, matching his cool reply. "But Vince has his own life and is making noises about retiring." He studied Jake's face. "And it all depends on what you decide."

"It's too early to make a decision."

"So just how are you planning to help the company?" Ryan asked tightly.

Jake gave him the once-over, only mildly surprised when the younger man, just like his sister, refused to break eye contact.

These Blackstones were tough.

"First, I need to get up to speed with all aspects of Blackstone Diamonds, starting with the financials and corporate structure. Then, I'll hold a meeting with the board and shareholders to reassure them of my commitment."

"Are you planning to commit?" Ric asked, leaning back in

his chair and crossing his arms. "Or are you going to break up the company after the shares stabilise?"

"How can I? I don't have a controlling interest."

"That's never stopped you before."

Jake studied Ric Perrini with renewed respect. If it came down to a vote, Matt Hammond held ten percent of the shares and had already pledged his support in Jake's favour. But that was purely because the man hated the Blackstones.

Jake didn't know these people. But he'd been in similar situations, ones that involved family, tradition and high emotion. You had to tread lightly. Be diplomatic. Get them onside with a small truth, at least.

"For now, I'm committed."

"That's not good enough," Garth snapped. "Howard built Blackstone's up from nothing. He wasn't a saint but he loved this company. He put his life into it, making it a successful, international brand name. His wish was to see that continue— with his family at the helm." The older man thumped the table with a clenched fist for emphasis. "After all these years, he never stopped believing you were alive somewhere. Even refused to put up a gravestone in your name. That's how damned stubborn and committed he was. And look—he was right. Don't you think you owe his memory—your family— more than a 'for now'?"

The impassioned speech made as much impact on Jake's composure as a feather on steel. He'd heard it all before, seen enough pleading, threatening and bargaining to not let it matter.

He held Buick in a cool stare until the older man let out a disgusted snort and settled back in his chair.

"A DNA test doesn't make a bunch of strangers suddenly family," Jake said calmly, ignoring the way Kim's face paled.

"I don't like this any more than you do. Make no mistake—this isn't about some newly discovered paternal ties to Howard Blackstone. I don't want or need the complication."

"So why are you doing it?" Ryan asked.

Jake smiled thinly. "To make money."

"You're a billionaire. How much more do you need?" Kim asked, her eyes astute.

Way too personal. Jake crossed his arms and met her gaze head-on. "Take my offer or not. You're quite welcome to maintain the status quo and let that press leak go unfound, watch the stock plummet, the shareholders pull out…"

"Or take our chances with you," Ric finished.

"Yep."

He rose to give them their thinking time and strode over to the cabinet to pour a glass of water. Unmindful of the hushed discussion at the other end of the room, he sipped slowly as he gazed upon the magnificent view of Sydney stretched in front of him, fixing on the familiar blue neon of his AdVance Corp across the bay, a physical manifestation of eight years' hard work.

He'd expected softer edges after Ryan's recent marriage, but the man's glare indicated a strong will. And, if the reports were true, an even stronger desire to prove himself in the face of Howard Blackstone's obvious preference for Ric Perrini. Just the sort of family infighting that jeopardised smart business decisions—which would, ironically, make his decision to keep them at arm's length that much easier.

For a week he'd immersed himself in this family—their history, their investments, even the salaciously unreliable gossip. He might be related to them on paper, but loyalty had to be earned. There were only four people in the world he trusted: His secretary. His chief of security. Quinn, who had voiced multiple warnings to watch his back. And his mother.

He didn't miss the irony. For someone with deep trust issues, he'd placed it with a woman who'd been living a lie.

"OK," Ric said at length. "Under one condition."

Jake turned his back to the window, placing his glass on the cabinet. "Which is?"

"No official announcements until we're good and ready."

Jake quirked an eyebrow. "And your reasoning is…?"

"You. The speculation alone will be enough to drop stock prices."

He smiled humourlessly. "And it conveniently stops anything from leaking out…unless one of you is the source."

Ryan visibly bristled, but Kim put a hand on his arm. "Your identity stays with us until we all agree on where and when to announce it," she said smoothly. "Not even the assistant we've assigned to you knows."

Great. A company mouthpiece to spout the latest platitudes about Blackstone's.

"Have you informed your solicitors and the private investigator?" Jake asked.

"We've called the P.I. off," Ric said.

Jake nodded. "So let's see what I can dig up on this leak before we start making anything official. A week, maybe two, should do it."

"Once people start seeing you here, it'll be hard to avoid speculation," Kimberley said.

"Which is why we've given you an office on the executive floor. Limited access. High security," Ric added.

"I don't need an office. But I will need complete access to your records."

"It's already done." Bitterness tinged Ryan's words. How much had it cost him to agree to that? For a brief second, Jake almost felt sorry for him. It disappeared when Ryan fixed him with a cold glare. He saw the enmity written in every muscle on the man's face.

"The only people who know the truth are family," Kimberley added.

Family. Jake's gut tightened at the word, but outwardly he just nodded.

"Vince will want to meet you," Kim said. "He's—"

"Howard's brother. Runs an opal mine in Coober Pedy. Lives in Adelaide and owns a ten-percent share. He's currently in the States on business."

"He's your uncle," Kim added calmly. "Then there's Sonya."

Jake heard the warmth in her voice, saw the emotion that briefly softened Kim's expression before she blinked it away.

An unfamiliar burst of injustice slammed into him, rendering him momentarily speechless. Sonya Hammond was a mother figure to these people. She was important.

He took a breath, quickly recovering with, "It's not necessary."

By the look on Kim's face he knew his response fell far short of acceptable. Well, hell. This wasn't exactly his dream situation, either.

Perrini said, "You'll have access to the internal filing and e-mail systems, plus a master key card to the building." He punched a number into the phone. "You understand that no files can leave the building, nor are there to be any unauthorised copies made."

"Naturally," Jake said smoothly.

Ric continued. "The elevator on the far right is executive

use only. It takes you to the basement, so there'll be no chance meetings with other staff. Your assistant, Holly McLeod, is outside."

I guess this means the meeting's over. "I'll need the current financials."

"I'll send them up," Ryan said curtly. He was the first to rise, striding over to the door and yanking it open. "Welcome to Blackstone's."

Holly McLeod waited as everyone exited the boardroom. Ryan, Ric and Garth were deep in discussion as they strode to the elevator. Nothing new there. They lived and breathed Blackstone Diamonds.

Then Jake Vance emerged and the seriousness of her predicament flipped her stomach.

It's nervousness. That's all.

He spotted her and gave a brief, humourless smile. "Miss McLeod."

Her softly murmured name tripped a breath of warm anticipation over her skin, one she quickly covered up by straightening the file in her arms. "Mr Vance—" she held out her hand "—I'm Holly McLeod. I'm to be your assistant for the duration of your stay."

When his long fingers wrapped around hers, her skin heated with the contact. It wasn't power he so clearly exuded. It was something much more seductive. Confidence? Control?

Intimacy.

The way his sharp green gaze swept her from head to toe, taking in her hair, her face, her business suit. The way those eyes probed hers until they finally came to rest on the small diamond solitaire at her throat.

She swallowed, withdrew and offered a key card, carefully avoiding his hand. "This will give you access to all the floors, plus the basement car park. You've been allocated a parking space for as long as you're with Blackstone's. I'll show you to your office now, if you like."

"No."

Holly blinked. "Sir?"

"It's Jake. I'm not staying." He stuck his hand in his suit jacket, pulled out a mobile phone and flipped it open. Without a second glance, he pocketed it. "You can give me a rundown of the company history in the car. Get the financials from Ryan Blackstone and I'll meet you in the basement."

She hesitated as he made short work of the corridor with his long, devouring strides. So he didn't want to view his domain, cast an all-encompassing powerful eye over the magnificent Sydney view. Of course. He had the mirror image from his North Sydney complex. Still, she'd anticipated questions, pulled all the relevant files and promotional material and put them on his desk. She'd made tentative meetings with department heads.

"Keep up, Miss McLeod," Jake said curtly as he pressed the elevator button.

Holly quickly regrouped and moved forward, apprehension giving way to irritation in the face of his cool perusal. "You're not authorised to remove files from the building, Mr Vance," she said shortly, refusing to flinch as his sharp eyes met hers. "But I'll go and personally make sure they're delivered up to your temporary office."

He scrutinised her with all the skill of a pro, but she returned his look steadily. *Oh, I know how you work, Mr Midas Touch.* The stare-down was part of his strategy, along with an emotionless, lay-out-the-facts style that most men grudgingly admired, despite his ruthless reputation. Men wanted to be him; women just wanted him. Period.

She pushed the elevator button repeatedly, tightening her grip on her file so it crushed up against her breasts like protective armour. "I think now's a good time to discuss how you'd like to work while you're here."

He frowned. "I don't expect you to be performing any personal assistant duties. I already have one."

"Holly is a wealth of information about Blackstone's. We're fortunate to have her," Kimberley said, from behind them. Holly ducked her gaze guiltily at the unexpected praise as Kim continued. "Make use of her expertise and gather as much knowledge as you can before deciding to invest with us."

Holly felt a confusing frisson of adversarial tension crackle between these two, like an argument was in the cards in the next two seconds. She'd never seen Kimberley be anything except utterly polite and professional, even to people she disliked.

Jake Vance, on the other hand, chose to do as he pleased, courtesy be damned.

"I need to speak to you later, Jake," Kimberley said pointedly.

"I can fit you in tomorrow."

"I'm flat out with Fashion Week but I can find time. I'll let Holly know." She gave up on the elevator and reached for the fire stairs door.

Jake turned to Holly when the door clicked shut, his face a study in controlled irritation. "It looks like I have myself an assistant, Miss McLeod." She blinked as he added, "As to how I work, it's quickly. I ask questions. You answer them. Simple."

She straightened her spine. "Do you have an agenda? A deadline or time frame that—"

"I plan on this taking no more than a week, ten days at the most. Every morning I'll decide on our timetable and we'll take it from there. I expect you to start work at eight and stay until everything that needs to get done is done. You need to work around my schedule and be available at my North Sydney office. Do you have other work commitments?"

She shook her head. "You're my first priority."

Holly watched in fascination as his sensuous mouth thinned, almost as if he were holding something back. His eyes, on the other hand, glittered for one second before he glanced away. "Let's start with the building layout and other assets." As if on cue, the doors pinged open and he swept his hand forward, indicating she go first.

"Our ground level is secured with high-end technology and a security desk, as you've seen," Holly began as they descended. "No employee gets in without their ID and a walk though the scanners. Visitors must be signed in and accompanied by an employee."

"What about the Blackstones themselves?"

"All executives are located on the forty-third floor with the rest of the board, and use this private elevator. Finance is on the thirty-fifth floor, PR on the twentieth. We also have an employee-only gym and health club, child-care center and cafeteria. We own the whole building, including the grand ballroom, shop fronts, bar and three restaurants that cover the ground, first and second floors facing George Street. Our employees get generous discounts at these and we have a standing table for executive use at each restaurant. We occasionally rent out our ballroom to other companies. Last year it was the B&S and Make a Wish Charity Ball."

She held out a glossy brochure that she'd helped design,

one that detailed the building's facilities. He just glanced at it, then back at her.

"No company propaganda. I prefer facts."

Right. Feeling as if she'd failed some kind of test, she tucked the offending material back into her folder. *Take a breath, Holly. Work out your strategy and stick with it.*

"The rest of the floors are taken up by HR, the press room and our other divisions."

"Which are?"

"Blackstone Jewellery, International Sales, Mining, Crafting and Design, Legal. I have a fact sheet of the departmental hierarchy and breakdown."

"I'll need that e-mailed."

She nodded and fixed her eyes on the descending numbers.

Jake crossed his arms and studied her profile before ending at the low, elegant sweep of dark hair that brushed past her ears and up into a stylish ponytail.

An unexpected stab of lust hit him low and hard, but with practised ease he stuffed it back. Still, it didn't stop his gaze from tripping back over her in leisurely study, taking in the navy suit that cinched in her waist, the V-neck shirt revealing a creamy throat adorned with one simple diamond on a gold chain. Down farther, her legs were encased in navy pants, ending in a pair of absurdly high sandals.

He found himself staring at those feet, the nails painted a subtle peach with the second toe sporting a diamond stud toe ring.

When she shifted the file in her arms and glanced over at him, he suddenly realised he'd been staring at the woman's feet.

He snapped his eyes up to meet hers and it hit him again. It wasn't the curve of her lips, nor the way her blue eyes tilted up at the corners. It was the tiny birthmark on the left side of her mouth, like some artist had painted it on to tease and tempt. To focus a man's attention.

A prime kissing target.

When she glanced away, her profile oozed cool professionalism. So why did that calm facade annoy him?

Jake was used to all the tricks when it came to business, but this was definitely a twist. They could've given him any old assistant, yet this gorgeous brunette's presence meant they'd obviously read the reports about Mia.

She was here not only to spy but to distract.

He scowled as his phone rang again. Expert, was she, held in high regard by Blackstone's? That was enough to give him pause.

He'd learned from his mistakes. If they thought a pair of cat's eyes and a kissy-mole would divert him from his purpose, they had another think coming. The press called him Mr Midas Touch, the bad boy of business, and if the Blackstones wanted an unfair fight, they would find out how bad he could be.

Two

So that was the great Jake Vance, Mr Midas Touch. Owner of the billion dollar AdVance Corp, corporate shark and Australia's third richest single man under forty.

Holly quickly dumped the financials on the desk of her temporary office, whirled out the glass doors and back to the elevators.

She'd been prepared for the arrogance, the intolerance of anyone he considered beneath him. He was unconventional, a risk taker. He made business decisions that wiser people labelled career suicide. But somehow he always managed to come out on top. Maybe because he gave the impression he had nothing to lose. Those who had nothing risked nothing.

But the Sunday feature article hadn't warned of the zing of attraction that had nearly floored her, the aura of power and control that stuck her tongue to the roof of her mouth and turned the words to dust in her throat.

Working at Blackstone's put her directly in the path of many powerful men. But Jake Vance…It was something in his face, the way his eyes had swept over her even as he tried to keep his perusal impersonal. Call her crazy, but she'd felt the air practically crackle with a weird sort of expectation.

The elevator doors swung open and she pressed the basement button impatiently.

Their gazes had locked just long enough for her to recognise the moment—predatory interest, an almost promissory flame in those deep green eyes. His mouth, a frankly sensual sculpture in warm flesh, had tweaked for a brief second, not enough to be called a smile.

Then he'd shut it down.

The only man in all her twenty-six years who'd forcibly smothered his interest.

No wonder he was at the top of his game. With that much control over his emotions, he was dark, brooding danger in an Italian designer suit. Heaven help a woman if the man ever genuinely smiled.

She curled her lip at the thought. Men in power—those who played God with people's lives—turned her blood cold.

Like Max Carlton, her soon-to-be ex-boss.

She'd been surprised when he'd approved her temporary transfer to PR eighteen months ago, but she'd had no time to worry if that approval came with strings, not when Blackstone's ten-year anniversary had been her top priority. Months later she'd been on the team organising Blackstone's Australian Fashion Week presence. It'd been a chance to show Kimberley Perrini her Blackstone's-funded studies were paying off, a chance she'd desperately wanted since graduating over a year ago. Then, last week, she'd been pulled from the glamorous event that was the ultimate dream of every Sydney designer to babysit Jake Vance.

She sighed, automatically brushing her hair back from her forehead. If only it were simply a babysitting job.

She finally arrived at the basement and found Jake standing beside a shiny silver Commodore, talking into his mobile phone.

She paused, taking in the perfect snapshot that oozed wealth and class, forcing her heart to slow down, to settle the stupid hitch in her breath. He looked up as she approached and, without pause, opened the back door for her.

Holly blinked. No limo? No uniformed driver? She slid into the creamy leather interior, a niggle of confusion creasing her brow.

Jake got in beside her, his phone call now finished. "Back to the office, Steve."

The car started with a gentle purr and the driver slid it into first gear, easing out the basement and into the traffic flow. And suddenly Holly realised Jake's attention was now focused solely on her.

Disturbingly focused attention in an even smaller space than the elevator.

She clicked on her seat belt, ignoring the way his green eyes grazed over her in concentrated study. When she'd first faced him it'd been a stretch to retain her composure. The natural command, the sheer sexuality he exuded had rocketed her pulse. Now in close, almost intimate, quarters, she felt the heated warmth curling up from her toes intensifying.

Here was a man used to getting his own way. He expected acquiescence, demanded it. He crushed anyone in his way.

"Besides the financials, what do you need?" She spoke calmly, that last thought aiding her steely resolve.

"How about you start with the Blackstone history?"

Holly gave him a curious look. "Anything specific?"

"Not particularly. Don't worry." His lips curved. "I'll stop you if it gets boring."

She blinked at his innocent expression. How could he make that neutral statement sound like such a sinful suggestion?

She concentrated on flicking through her documents to stop herself from flushing. Boring and Jake Vance were planets apart. Of that she was certain.

As Holly talked, Jake listened, carefully analysing not only her words, but her nonverbal cues. As they drove onto Sydney Harbour Bridge he noticed the way her eyes lit up when she recounted the intriguing history of the Blackstones. He knew all this, thanks to his research team. But it was more interesting hearing it from her lips than reading a dry hundred-page report. He asked questions and she expanded on the details, providing answers without hesitation. She knew her stuff.

Yeah, she's smart and attractive. But she works for Blackstone's.

He'd been blindsided twice before. Lucy had ripped out his heart when he'd needed her support the most. Seven years later, Mia had used her position as his assistant to violate his trust. He'd quickly learned a harsh lesson: To ensure his utmost privacy, no one was permitted to breach his tight security measures. His company had the strictest security checks, his private life had triple that. It just wasn't worth everything he'd worked his whole life for.

"Unlike other jewellers, Blackstone's issues only two glossies every year."

Focus. One second was all he needed to clear his mind, one second to shove his memories back into the past and concentrate on the here and now.

"Two catalogues," he repeated.

Holly nodded. "October and January."

"No Christmas issue?"

"No. Valentine's Day is our busiest time. We found our clients started shopping for Christmas as early as October. A Blackstone diamond is an investment. It signals superior quality and workmanship, something that women aspire to have, combined with the Australian mystique of the outback. Our branding says it all: the simple use of the word 'heart.' Some of our previous campaigns were 'heart felt,' 'heart's desire' and 'from the heart.' This is our most recent issue." She flipped open her folder. Jake gave it a cursory glance and focused on another magazine on the seat.

"What's that?"

Holly glanced down. "Our first issue. A collector's item, actually. There are only twenty existing copies in the world. That's Howard and Ursula. She's wearing the Blackstone Rose."

Unable to help himself, Jake slowly reached for the copy and stared at the cover. Looking every inch its 1976 date, the slim glossy brochure showed a candid but spectacular shot of a young couple in formal evening dress on the steps of the Sydney Opera House. Howard Blackstone in a tux, his wolfish smile triumphant. On his arm, Ursula was dressed in a strapless floor-length creation, her hair piled up into a then-fashionable beehive. The necklace around her neck was large and ostentatious, everything spectacular and showy that he'd come to expect from Howard Blackstone. There were five diamonds—four round stones with a teardrop shaped one dangling in the center. It sat high and heavy on Ursula's neck like a collar, a symbol of ownership.

The look in Ursula's face confirmed his impression. She was deeply unhappy. Sure, she smiled, but there was no joy behind it, the emotion in her eyes dull and resigned.

She had wealth, beauty and fame. Surely these things should have made her ecstatic, not miserable.

"When was this taken?"

"December 1976."

Two months after he'd been stolen. No wonder she looked miserable. And Howard, being the self-absorbed bastard he was, had probably convinced her to dress up and show off the diamonds anyway.

Despite himself, his chest tightened. Dammit. He dropped the magazine with a scowl, cursing himself for allowing that small weakness to take up space in his head. Emotion and business did not mix.

Holly's low, husky voice suddenly broke through and with the effort it took to flip a switch, he refocused. He turned back to face her, his face expressionless, as she continued.

"The Blackstone Rose came from a diamond called the Heart of the Outback. Jeb Hammond—that's Ryan and Kimberley's grandfather and Howard's father-in-law—gifted the stone to his daughter Ursula to celebrate the birth of James Blackstone, his first grandchild, in 1974. Howard then had it made into the Blackstone Rose necklace the following year." She paused. "Do you know much about diamonds?"

"Aren't they a girl's best friend?"

She gave him a smile that struck him as slightly patronizing. "Not this one."

"I thought every woman liked diamonds."

"I'm more of a sapphire girl," she admitted coolly. She shifted and straightened her back against the leather seat. "Diamonds are commonly judged by the 'four Cs'—cut, clarity, color and carat. The cut—"

"Determines its brilliance. Most gemmologists consider cut the most important diamond characteristic."

"Yes. There's no single measurement to define it…" Holly stopped. "But you're best mates with Quinn Everard. You probably know this already."

He nodded. "Some. Go on."

"Am I being graded on this?" She frowned. "Because if you're not happy with the information I'm giving you—"

"I am, Holly," he said curtly. "Please continue." After the briefest of pauses, she turned the page and showed him a studio shot of the Blackstone Rose sitting elegantly on black velvet. The camera flash had captured the reflection against one of the stone's polished surfaces, creating a starry burst of light.

He'd never understood the female obsession with jewellery but these were… "Impressive. The Blackstone Rose necklace was stolen on Ursula's thirtieth birthday, right?"

"It went missing around that time," she corrected him.

Jake eased his long legs forward, crossing them at the ankles. "A moot point now they've been found. For whatever reason, Howard bequeathed the stones to Marise, and now that she's dead, they're Matt Hammond's."

Holly paused at the mention of Matt. She'd read about the long-standing Blackstone-Hammond feud like everyone else, had pored over the numerous articles about their complicated history with a mixture of sadness and amazement. Matt's father and Kimberley's mother were brother and sister, yet because of greed, power and jealousy, the branches of the family tree had grown acres apart.

With a frown, Holly recalled the last few months that had been publicly played out in the media. Whatever the families' grievances, Matt didn't deserve to have his dead wife linked with notorious womaniser Howard Blackstone, to have her die in Howard's plane crash off the Pacific coast. His son Blake didn't deserve to have the memory of his mother tainted by salacious gossip.

Jake waited for her to comment, to echo what the press had feverishly dubbed the "Howard-and-Marise affair", but she remained silent. "And…?" he finally prompted.

"And what?" she replied calmly. "Look, Mr Vance, I'm not entirely sure what you want to know—"

"Dynamics."

"Sorry?"

"I'm interested in family dynamics. The mark of a success-ful family company depends on that family working together in a harmonious environment."

"The Blackstones have grown and thrived for over thirty years. You can't get more successful than that."

"It's not about monetary success. It's about respect, both for each other and their employees."

"What makes you think they don't have respect?"

"Howard Blackstone was a dictator. That much I do know. He was petty, vengeful and treated his employees and family like crap. He also relied on cronyism to stay on top of the heap." He suddenly leaned forward and Holly instinctively pulled back. "What I want to know is why people continued to work with him if he was such a bastard?"

Her eyes flashed, the first real display of anger escaping

her cool businesslike facade. "I don't know. Why do people still work for you?"

The air stilled.

Holly's breath hitched as her stomach plummeted. She'd done it now, offended the great Jake Vance to the soles of his imported leather shoes. With a pounding heart, she braced herself for the icy reprimand, a potent display of authority designed to put her right back into her place. Instead…

He smiled.

And what a smile it was.

Amusement creased his eyes, softening his jawline and bringing forth a dimple to his cheek. A dimple. As if the man didn't have enough swooning power over the female population. It transformed his striking, almost harsh, features into something warm and touchable.

"I find it very interesting," he murmured, "that I irritate you so much. Is it about the way I do business?"

"No," she lied.

"So it's personal."

She blinked nervously. He was close but not close enough to invade her space. Yet she could sense the warmth from his broad, impeccably suited body, the single-minded focus as his eyes freely roamed over her face, coming to rest at a spot dangerously close to her mouth.

She tried to swallow but it felt like dust clogged her throat. "I'm just here to do my job, Mr Vance."

"Really."

His scepticism irritated: it was obvious he trusted her as much as she did him. Still, she met his considering look with one of her own, willing calm into every inch of her humming body. "Yes. Shall we get back to your investment, Mr Vance?"

"Jake." In an echo of his movements in the Blackstone's basement, he pulled his phone out and checked the screen. "I need to know how the family interacts," he said as he pushed a few buttons. "I'm not going to invest in Blackstone's if they can't control their in-fighting. And then there's Matt Hammond, a man who's publicly and repeatedly voiced his hatred of Blackstone's and who now owns ten percent of the shares."

Holly paused, see-sawing between honesty and loyalty. This was another test. He already knew the answers but wanted to see how far she'd go.

Damn the man.

"You know the Hammonds and Blackstones have a long and tragic history," she said tightly to his impassive face. "Yes, Marise used to work for Blackstone's. Yes, she married into the one family Howard despised. And on her death—"

"Ursula's jewellery and diamonds went to Matt and Marise's son, Blake." Almost as if bored with the interrogation, he studied the passing traffic as they exited the Harbour Bridge. "But one diamond's still out there."

"Still lost," Holly conceded, stopping before she added, *just like James Blackstone.*

Lost.

A strange shiver brushed over Jake's skin, like the fingers of a dead woman grazing his conscience.

A lost diamond. A missing Blackstone.

The awful comparison sneaked into his head and lingered as he absently rubbed his arm where his so-called mother had dug in her fingers, the death grip from that frail hand suddenly sharp, astute.

Don't hate me, Jake. Her eyes had taken on a fevered

quality, wide in her sunken face. *I wanted you so much. I love you more than anything.*

And now here he was. Not lost any more. So why did he still feel like some shipwreck survivor adrift on the sea?

Two hours later, a pregnant Jessica Cotter Blackstone had met Jake and Holly at the back door to the exclusive Blackstone's Sydney store and guided them to a private showing room.

Holly shifted in her chair and recrossed her legs. Up until now, she'd always liked this room for its ample, airy space. But with Jake sitting so close, even the long glass-topped mahogany display table wasn't sufficient to ward off the strange little buzzes zapping her body.

She glanced to her right, to the huge photo of Briana Davenport above a display cabinet. Dubbed the Face of Blackstone's, the model was glancing into the camera over one shoulder, a sensual smile on her lips, drop diamonds shining from her ears, matching the sparkle in her gorgeous eyes. Holly had seen Jessica look at the picture when they'd first arrived, then apologetically at Jake. He'd merely shrugged, but Holly had watched the way his attention lingered on the stunning face of his former flame.

She shook her head. The man had dated practically every available, gorgeous socialite in Sydney. He was a confirmed bachelor. A confirmed serial dater, her all-knowing flatmate Miko would say with a toss of her jet-black hair. Jake had proved her rich man–supermodel theory in spades when he'd taken up with Briana. With the press alluding to marriage at one stage, it must have cut the man's ego deeply when she'd thrown him over for millionaire lawyer Jarrod Hammond who was also, ironically, Matt Hammond's brother. Jake had been suspiciously absent from the spotlight in the weeks that followed…unlike the Blackstones, with their undeserved trials and tribulations.

More than once her mind had lingered on the comparison between AdVance Corp and Blackstone's. Just like Howard, Jake Vance had started from nothing. But where Jake was a lone wolf, Howard Blackstone and his family had created a dream, nurturing it into the multibillion-dollar business it was today. Despite that success, people had loved to hate Howard Blackstone. There was that something in Jake Vance, too, something that made her quake. It was the same ruthlessness, the cold look in their eyes. Even Max, with his skilled ability to diffuse the most volatile of arguments, wasn't exempt from Howard's displeasure. And like Howard, once crossed, nothing short of total destruction would satisfy Jake Vance. She had no doubt if you incurred the man's displeasure, you'd know about it.

So what will he do to you when he finds out you're nothing more than a corporate spy?

Her heart, already pounding with nervousness, started to throb in earnest. *If he found out. If.*

Jessica finally returned with a velvet tray and Holly determinedly ignored the flutter of helplessness starting in her belly. Instead, she watched Jake, who was concentrating intently on Jessica as she explained the cutting process, the rarity of pink diamonds and alluvial deposits. When she referenced something in the store brief she'd prepared, he looked down at the document and Holly became all too well aware of his hair as it slid over his forehead. It was too long to be called a military cut, too short to be completely unconventional.

It looked clean. Shiny. She resisted the sudden urge to lean forward and sniff. Instead she remained still, only half-surprised that her breath quivered on the way in.

His tall, commanding presence, so supremely confident in an expensive dark grey suit, had her itching to scoot her chair back to the outer edges of her comfort zone. He might be an arm's length away, but she was too close to escape the aura that radiated from him like some kind of will-numbing drug.

Jake shook off the tiny prickles of sensation from Holly's scrutiny and deliberately focused on the tray of diamonds before him. As Jessica turned a huge yellow-stoned ring deftly into the light, it created a kaleidoscope of rainbow shards across the room. So this was the fuel for Howard's obsession. If he'd been hoping for answers in the multifaceted polished depths, he was disappointed.

"Blackstone's is famous for our candies," Jessica said, replacing the ring and picking up a blue-stoned bracelet set in silver. "Pale-canary to deep-sun yellow. Pinks, blues, greens. If I know Holly, she's already told you about our wares."

Jake zoomed back in on his too-silent assistant and directed his question at her. "How much are pink diamonds worth?"

He noted the way she shoved back her hair, the jerky movement containing an underlying tension. Yet her eyes were as sharp and clear as the gemstones he'd been viewing. "At a 2004 Sotheby's auction, a 351 round 1.23 intense purplish pink went for just over a hundred and forty-three thousand dollars a carat. Minimum bids started at a hundred thousand dollars a carat."

"So something like—say, the Blackstone Rose, would be...?"

"The four round trillion-cut diamonds were seven carats

each, the pear-shape center, ten. At the time it was worth millions. Today…who knows?"

The cool and matter-of-fact way she imparted that information intrigued him. He'd never known a woman to be so calm when discussing the glorious brilliance of a priceless gem. She'd been more into Blackstone history than what made Howard a dizzying financial success.

In the small space of a day she'd piqued his interest, both physically and mentally.

"Try it on." Jessica grinned at Holly, forcing Jake's attention back to the tray of diamonds spread before him like party trinkets.

When Holly smiled he got the feeling this was a familiar scenario for the two women. He watched her finger the blue sapphire solitaire, running her thumb pad almost reverently over the square gem on a gold band, surrounded by tiny diamonds. In the background, Jake heard Jessica recounting some statistics about diamond mining but, at this moment, Holly commanded his attention.

Slowly, sensuously, she slid the ring over her knuckle, until it came to rest at the base of her finger.

An image burst forth, unwilling, unbidden. Holly wearing that ring and not much else.

His throat suddenly became drier than the Great Sandy Desert.

"That's bad luck, you know," he murmured. Her eyes shot to his as he clarified. "Putting a ring on your wedding finger without a proposal."

She paused, obviously testing her retort, until Jessica answered with a laugh. "Don't tell me you believe in old wives' tales, Jake?"

"My mum swore by them."

Jessica's expression turned sympathetic. "I'm sorry about your mother."

He waved her apology away and instead picked up a pink diamond.

Holly quickly placed the ring back on the tray as her senses registered the faint teasing smell of Jake's cologne. She didn't want to look, shouldn't look, but somehow, she found herself engulfed in those intelligent green eyes. Too eagerly, her body leaped in response. Warmth started in the pit of her belly, heating as it unfurled and spread. *Oh, my.*

His eyes skimmed her face, betraying nothing but cool perusal. If she hadn't seen the spark of heat in his eyes that morning, she would've said he was a damn robot.

Do not think about that. Think about your mission.

She followed his movements as he picked up one stone, then another. Yeah, she was a regular Mata Hari all right, trying to uncover the deep dark secrets of Mr Midas Touch himself. As if she'd find anything that wasn't already in the public domain.

As if there'd be anything out there he hadn't already personally vetted and approved.

The problem was, she realised as they left the store, Jake was rapidly becoming so not what she'd expected. He'd greeted the heavily pregnant Jessica warmly, pulling over a comfy one-seater for her instead of the harder official viewing chairs. He'd silently flicked through Jessica's brief of the store, asked intuitive questions about the stones and the staff. And why had he wanted to see the diamonds? It didn't matter what a bunch of gemstones looked like. It was Blackstone's ability to make money that mattered. If selling cow dung turned a profit the man would be interested.

She stared out the car window, at the mounting peak-hour traffic. She needed to remember that Jake Vance was a ruthless man. She'd read about his famed decisiveness, his superior negotiation skills, all borne from his meteoric rise from the ashes following false accusations from Jaxon Financial's CEO. One interviewer in particular wasn't impressed by Jake's success, labelling him as "autocratic, cold and poisonously polite."

Jake had the ability to destroy people in so many different ways that it took her breath away. That should be enough to turn her off. So why did her brain have to act so damn… *female* when he was around?

As if sensing her thoughts, he glanced at her.

Their gazes clashed and for a second she felt a brief flicker of scalding heat before— Yep, there came the shutdown just before he returned to the brief.

Now he was just plain irritated. As if she was the last person in the world he wanted to see.

Yeah, I know how that feels.

Her phone suddenly rang, cutting off her thoughts.

With a soft groan, she noted the number. "I need to take this. Excuse me." Without waiting for Jake's acquiescence, she angled herself towards the window and took the call.

Minutes later, as her mother's bank manager spelled out the dire straits of her predicament, Holly's stomach dipped. The brief feeling of nausea was quickly followed by an irrational wave of injustice. Here she was, in the midst of almost obscene wealth, while her parents were struggling with the fallout of one stupid business decision.

The faint tinge of guilt roiled in her stomach as she clicked off the call. If only she hadn't been a typically selfish teenager, nagging her parents to sell… But now she had to be the strong one and take care of them.

Her breath came out in a whoosh. *I need to keep my job, which means spying on Jake Vance.*

She stared out the window, at the passing traffic along George Street, a constant reminder of the realities of who she was and what she'd done and what she needed to do to keep her reputation and her family safe.

Jake stared at the document on his lap until he realised he'd been reading the same paragraph five times. During her mystery call, he'd noticed her tense and bow her head. After a few hushed whispers, she'd shoved a hand through her hair and paused. He caught "money," "payment" and "default" before she finally hung up.

Suspicion arrowed through him like a bolt from heaven. He opened his mouth to say something but suddenly pulled himself short. Her shoulders were hunched in a position he'd seen too many times before. Defeat.

He caught a faint sound. A sigh? No. It was a shuddery intake, almost as if she were trying to draw strength on a breath but failing abysmally. That small vulnerability, hitting below the belt and tightening his chest in a fierce irrational rush of emotion threw him for a six.

Against all logical reasoning, he lifted a hand, but just as quickly, he forced it back to the brief with a thump.

His small movement shattered the air and Holly whirled. "Sorry about that." She shoved away a stray curl as the now-familiar polite smile spread her mouth briefly. "Where were we?"

"Your hair."

"What?"

He flicked a finger towards her head. "Your clip's come loose."

"Oh."

She yanked back her hair, a gentle flush spreading across the high curves of her cheeks. Jake couldn't hide his amusement, which faltered when a sudden unbidden thought flashed through his head. *How would she look, hair loose and spread out on my pillow?*

At the store, when she had picked up that blue ring, he'd seen a glimpse of something in her gaze. Longing. Wanting. As if she desperately needed but knew she couldn't have.

His attention flickered back over her face, taking in her profile, that small mole hidden from his view. There was nothing he couldn't have. Nothing he'd been denied.

Desire cleaved his gut, sharp and urgent. Despite the tight rein on his control, he smiled.

It was a smile bereft of humour. A smile full of grudging admission.

He wanted Holly. At least, his body wanted her and generally, what he wanted, he got. But this time…

After years of business decisions based on a combination of solid facts and honed sixth sense, his gut feeling failed him right now. And in the absence of that, he had to go with what his past had taught him.

Stay away.

"It's after five. I'll take you home," he said curtly.

She shook her head. "That won't be necessary."

"It's not a problem."

Holly crossed her arms with a soft sigh, realising arguing would be futile in the face of his cool determination.

Ten minutes later, they were in front of her apartment

building and he'd rounded the car to open her door. When he offered his hand, she hesitated only briefly before taking it.

Bad decision, she told herself. Bad, bad, bad.

After he helped her exit she just stood there, her fingers still engulfed in his. He commanded her attention, unwillingly, effortlessly.

If the May night air held a chill, Holly couldn't feel it. Instead, the heat of him sucked all the breath from her lungs, leaving her heart jumping merrily along in anticipation. He was staring down at her with those piercing, almost analytical eyes, their bodies too close for her comfort. For one insane second, the romantic in her imagined him leaning in for a goodbye kiss on the cheek but she quickly dismissed the fanciful thought with a blink. *Didn't stop you wanting it, though, did it?*

She eased her hand from his warm grip and just like that, the moment shattered. As he stepped back, the night air whooshed into the void, sending a shiver over her skin.

"What's your phone number?" he asked.

"Why?"

Amusement tweaked his lips into a shadowy smile. "In case I need to call you."

She felt the hot flush of embarrassment across her cheeks as she reeled off her mobile number and he punched it into his phone.

"Steve will pick you up at seven tomorrow. We'll be flying to an appointment in Lighting Ridge," Jake said, pocketing his phone. At her look of confusion, he added, "To check on a new complex I'm building."

"You don't delegate?"

"Some things I choose not to." He leaned against the car,

a nonchalant gesture that oddly suited him. "Have a good night, Holly."

Jake watched as she walked up the pathway to her apartment, her back ramrod straight, her hips swaying in that deliciously tantalizing way. When she unlocked the door, turned to him with a nod and disappeared inside, his smile fled.

It was time to find out just who Holly McLeod was.

Three

"The crisis center was your mother's idea," Holly casually stated as they boarded the Cessna on their way back to Sydney the next afternoon.

"Yes," he said, nodding to the flight attendant and handing him his coat.

"I'm sorry for your loss, Mr Vance."

He'd heard those simple words a thousand times in the past few weeks, yet instinctively he knew Holly meant them.

"My mother was committed to causes," he acknowledged as he eased into the black leather seat.

"So I heard. You must have been very proud of her." He gave a non-committal answer then said, "Better strap yourself in." She nodded and went to her seat further down the aisle.

Pride wasn't the first thing that came to mind when he thought of April Vance Kellerman these days. He'd buried her last month, what now seemed a lifetime ago. Unbidden, the past crowded his head with the suppressed memories his mother's shocking confession had stirred to the surface. An urgent, whispered confession that he'd put down to the painkillers. The confession of a dying woman who'd been living a lie. One that had suddenly taken on malevolent form.

The only reason she'd confessed was fear—fear of being discovered. If Howard's investigator hadn't been so dogged in his pursuit, crossing state lines on the strength of speculation and hearsay to finally end up in Jake's hometown, he had no doubt he'd still be in the dark about his true parentage.

He balled a fist and thumped it gently on the cold glass window. Like water from a cracked cup, the resentment seeped out, leaving a deep, dark emptiness in its wake.

Everything he knew, everything he'd based his life on was a lie. Yet so many things, so many oddities he'd never questioned clicked into place: Why they'd lived like nomads, shifting across state lines. Why family was never mentioned. And the nightmares that had finally stopped when he was ten years old.

Jake sighed and allowed himself that moment of grief and guilt. The two powerful emotions mingled to form a hard black lump in his gut. If he took any more time, he'd be forced to look long and hard at every choice, every decision April had made that had shaped his life.

Reluctantly he acknowledged a simple fact: April's death had hit way too close to home. He'd already begun to reassess his life after her funeral, to silently question just who he was and what he was doing. The inevitable shadows of death had touched him deeply, the painful, scary vulnerability it wreaked forcing him to re-evaluate his ten-year plan.

That plan was close to completion: he had everything money could buy and then some. Everything the Blackstones had been born into, everything April had lacked. After this Blackstones fiasco was behind him, he could fully commit to the last on his list—get himself a wife and start a family.

He glanced back to Holly. She was staring out the window with a pair of headphones on, studiously concentrating on the tarmac as they taxied down the runway. And just like that, his whole body tightened, forcing a surprised breath from his throat.

With mounting irritation he silently admitted his plan to intimidate her—and by default, the Blackstones—with an overt display of wealth had backfired. He'd wanted Blackstone's to be clear on exactly who they were dealing with, and what he could do if crossed. But it surprised him how calmly she took everything in her stride, from the early flight in his top-of-the-line ten-seater Cessna to his subtle commands that had them winging their way back to Sydney a few hours later. She hadn't missed a beat, answering his blunt questions with accuracy, waiting patiently while he signed off on the multiplex center.

This girl from the bush fit right into his million-dollar world as if born to it. And she was tempting, his little Blackstone's assistant, with her snug business skirts and touch-me shirts. His groin ached in sudden painful remembrance of last night. She'd invaded his dreams and got under his skin in a way other women hadn't. It was part desire, part knowledge of the unknown. Was she a spy? Did she have an agenda? Perversely, not knowing excited him even more.

He scowled, looking but not seeing the runway flash by as they picked up speed and launched into the air with a flourish.

If he wasn't careful, his fascination would become a weakness. He'd been stupid enough to allow one woman to break his heart then let another destroy his trust. It wasn't going to happen again.

But damn, he wanted her. Probably, he admitted ruefully, because he shouldn't have her.

His phone rang then, dragging him from those dangerous thoughts.

"How did it go with the Blackstones?" said Quinn by way of greeting.

"How do you think?" Jake muttered, resting the phone on his shoulder while shuffling through the floor plans of the center he'd just inspected. "The DNA sealed it. And now I have a walking, talking Blackstone's billboard to keep tabs on me while giving the hard sell." He eased back in his seat and the leather squeaked in protest.

"Is she cute?"

"Does it matter?" Jake scowled.

"Which means she is."

"So?"

"A guy just needs to know these things."

The tension in Jake's shoulders relaxed an inch. "Right. You're getting soft in your old age, mate," he drawled, his attention fixed out the window, at the huge expanse of drought-stricken land rolling below.

"There's more to life than making money."

"Ahh, another piece of Quinn-wisdom. Next you'll be telling me 'all you need is love.'"

"Maybe all you need is your hot little Blackstone's billboard."

Jake snorted. "Forgotten Mia, have you?"

"Everyone else has. But hey, if you're happy dragging that baggage around with you—"

"I don't have baggage."

"Right." Quinn's frustration crackled down the line. "Lucy. Your stepdad. All those shitty little towns you grew up in. You've got a whole bloody wardrobe, mate."

"Yeah, thanks for that." Jake screwed up his eyes and rubbed the back of his neck. "While I have you here, is there any way of tracking down that missing Blackstone diamond?"

"I'll get onto it straight after I finish building my time machine."

"Smart-ass."

"Laser identification wasn't invented until the early eighties. You'd have a better chance finding Eldorado. And anyway, Matt Hammond…already…me…it."

Jake frowned. "You're breaking up."

The line went dead and with a soft curse, Jake hung up.

Suddenly restless, he rose to his feet and walked the few metres down the plane to where Holly was now studiously scribbling on a spreadsheet.

When he approached she glanced up and quickly shoved a folder across the papers, but not before he caught the heading on the top. Finances.

"A bit early for your tax return," he said mildly, and leaned against the back of seat, crossing his arms.

"I like to get on top of things." She met his eyes almost defiantly and changed the subject. "I've been organising your schedule," she said without preamble. "You've got a four-o'clock meeting with Kimberley, and I've asked our department heads for their last quarterly reports." She offered some papers to him. "I printed out the corporate structure, along with the contact numbers of key Blackstone personnel. After five I'll give you a proper tour of the building."

He stood there, filling the space too well, looking far too comfortable, Holly thought with chagrin. When he leaned in to take the documents, awareness suddenly hit. He smelled warm, musky and expensive. He smelled wonderful.

She surreptitiously glanced at her watch, trying to hide her nervousness, but he caught her look.

"Would you like to join me for lunch?"

His mild question hung in the air but she swore she could see a faint flicker of challenge in his eyes. Ruthlessly she ground out a stab of desire. "No, thank you."

He raised one brow. "Why not?"

"Because I brought my own."

"You'd rather brown bag it than have a proper meal with me?"

She paused, weighing her answer. "Yes."

His short chuckle surprised her. "It's just food, Holly. We'll use a Blackstone's restaurant. And talk business."

She tipped her head, considering him. "Hasn't anyone ever told you no?"

"Not if they wanted to keep their job."

She bristled. "You'd sack me for refusing to eat with you?"

"No." His answering grin did nothing to ease her tension. "Anyway, I can't sack you. You work for Blackstone's."

"And you want to eat with me…why?"

"Maybe I just want your company."

Holly gave an inward groan at the seductive smile stretching his sinful mouth. He might be gorgeous, but she forced herself to remember who he was. Her boss. At least for now.

Regardless of how she felt, she had to see this through.

It'd do no good to stuff this up, not when she'd been backed into a corner.

She gave a curt, imperious nod, not wanting to appear too willing. "Let me make a call."

An hour later they were guided to a private table at the back of Si Ristorante, one of Blackstone's first-floor eateries.

"I'm surprised you have time for lunch, given your schedule," Holly said as the waiter brought them menus.

"I always make time to eat. Good food and a bottle of wine predispose people to generosity. And I also have a weakness for—" his gaze skimmed over her face, settling on a spot a little left to her mouth "—gnocchi."

Flustered, she busied herself with pouring a glass of water from the carafe. "And do you always treat your employees?"

"Who said I'm paying?"

Holly snapped up her eyes to meet his amused ones, and for one incredible second it felt like the world had stopped spinning.

Silly girl, Holly thought dazedly as she looked into those emerald eyes, the edges creased with uncharacteristic humour. The man had a billion reasons to smile, yet not one press clipping showed him happy. Dark, brooding or scowling, yes. Smiling? No.

I wonder why.

"Did you always want to work at Blackstone's?" he asked casually, changing the heated direction of her thoughts.

"No." She took his lead and studied the menu too. "But jobs are hard to come by out west so I moved."

"Where are you from?"

She hesitated, contemplating the wisdom of giving too much information. "You won't know it."

"Try me."

"Kissy Oak." She flushed as his eyes focused on her lips for a second. "It's a small farming community a few miles west of Dubbo."

"A small-town girl," he said softly. "Did you leave any small-town boys behind?"

"Why do you need to know?"

"Just making small talk. Getting to know my assistant."

When he smiled with deliberate charm, Holly's suspicion deepened. The man obviously knew the effect he had on women. Just not this woman.

"Don't you know already, thanks to your crack research team?"

His expression turned shrewd. "Reports don't tell me everything."

She noted the pointed absence of an outright denial and crossed her arms, trying to keep a firm hold on her mounting irritation. "So *you* tell me."

To his credit, he looked her straight in the eye and said calmly, "You were born on the thirtieth of April, 1982 in Dubbo Hospital to Martin and Maureen McLeod. Your twin brother, Daniel, died two days later. Your parents owned McLeod Crop Dusting, serving the farming communities around Dubbo. When you were seventeen, MacFlight bought them out then went bust. You moved to the city, started at Blackstone's in Human Resources and have just finished a Blackstone's-funded degree at university. Your official position is PA to the Human Resources Manager but you're currently filling a temp position with PR. Your mother is living on a government pension and your father on disability."

Holly sucked in a breath as she shut the menu with deliberate slowness. How neatly he'd summed up the emotional roller coaster of her life, explaining away the past nine years without sensation or feeling. But she knew better. Jake couldn't know the gut-wrenching hours at hospital, comforting her hysterical mother while waiting for her dad to come out of intensive care following a stroke. Then the months of expensive rehab, no longer covered by their expired health insurance. The day-to-day living expenses of food, electricity, rates. She'd wrestled with the worry and stress every day until it was a permanent throb of duty lodged in a tiny corner of her heart.

She flushed when she was angry, Jake noticed absently, watching the heat coloring her cheeks a soft shade of pink. And unfortunately, he also realised that her precarious financial situation put her right at the top of his list of suspects for the press leak.

She flicked her eyes away, sweeping the restaurant to study the lunch crowd. But the calculated move couldn't detract from the struggle he could see warring on her features.

He knew she was aware of his scrutiny. And when he saw her fingers go to her earlobe and fiddle with the diamond stud there, he smiled. She wasn't just angry. She was nervous. *Interesting*.

"You were working while studying part-time at Shipley University," he stated.

To her credit, she tempered her annoyance with a small nod. "Business Management and Marketing."

"You were profiled in the university's journal as an exceptional talent," he said, "after handling that 'sex for grades' scandal last year."

"That's right."

"So why didn't you take the university's job offer instead?"

Holly blinked. "Blackstone's paid for my education. Why would I take another job? Besides, the university is—" she paused, picking her words with care "—conservative. Dress code, morality clauses—"

"Blackstone's has a morality clause," Jake interjected.

"But only for employees working within the same department. And the pay is more, the opportunities to advance much greater. I also like working here."

His gaze became speculative. "Working full-time and going to university part-time must've played hell with your social life."

"No. I focused on work."

Jake nodded. "So what made you volunteer to assist me?"

"I didn't. I got seconded."

Ahh. Jake placed the menu on his plate. Despite her denials, she was pissed. Enough for a little payback? He did the math in his head. No. The leak had been going on since Christmas, which meant something had happened just before Howard's plane went down.

The waiter arrived to take their orders then, but after the man left, the silence continued.

Determined not to let the unnerving intensity of Jake's study affect her, Holly reached for the bread basket—at exactly the same time Jake did.

Her mouth dropped from the shock of their skin-on-skin contact, her eyes widening. To recover from that surprising little zing, she yanked her hand back.

And there it was again. Why couldn't she shake the feeling

that one day, somehow, if he had his way, they'd be more than boss and assistant?

"Can I ask you something?" she said suddenly.

He eased back in his chair and picked up the water goblet. "You can. But I might not answer."

"How long will you be here?" *How long before I can get my job back, when I can resume a normal life…and I can stop my stomach flipping every time you study me like I'm a particularly interesting puzzle that needs to be unravelled?*

His smile turned mockingly sensual. "In a hurry to get back to Human Resources?"

"No. I'm waiting on my transfer papers to PR."

He paused for a second, his gaze holding her defiant one. In the next, a grudging smile teased his lips.

Holly nearly groaned aloud. Oh, man. The warmth of that one simple smile scorched her like she'd been caught in the pathway of a comet. The heated aftermath spread from her fingertips to the bottom of her black Jimmy Choos, heat of a purely female nature. His smile, combined with the warmth in his voice, was deliberately calculated to disarm her. There wasn't a woman he couldn't charm if he put his mind to it. She'd already witnessed it with Jessica.

Bad, bad move. You don't even like the guy.

Jake watched her fiddle with the stud in her ear again. "You've got something to say," he said casually.

She stilled. "Mr Vance…"

"Jake. It's Jake."

"Jake." She paused, which only heightened the way his name sounded on her lips. Lips that were painted a luscious shade of berry, so very close to that little kissy-mole.

"Kimberley's brief said you're looking to invest in Blackstone's. But I thought AdVance Corp was all about…" She paused, searching for the right word.

"Conquer and divide?" Jake smiled thinly, toying with the stem of his glass. "Don't believe everything you read. I like to see what I'm getting before I invest, to decide if it's worthy of my time and money." At least, that part had started out true. But after last night, when he'd dissected the deeper implications for the tenth time, he'd realised one thing. He was a Blackstone. Just because he hadn't had the privilege of the name for the last thirty-two years didn't mean he should let a successful corporate entity crumble to the ground. He wasn't seventeen any more, running away from the shame of his past. The story wasn't going away and it was within his power to save this company.

Now he said, "I'm looking to expand my options. Blackstone's is an important part of Australian corporate history but has been floundering since January. It's a perfect choice."

"So you have no intention of breaking us up?"

Us. Not "Blackstone's" or "the company". *Us*. As if she was part of a family. His gut clenched. "Hadn't even entered my mind."

The doubt written so clearly on her face got his back up. "Afraid of losing your job, Holly?"

"It's more than just a job to me." She focused on straightening the already perfect cutlery. For one second, Jake thought about defending himself with the truth, but just as quickly reined himself in.

"You don't like me. Why?"

Her head snapped up, showing him a glimpse of something simmering just below the surface. Yet her reply was one in studied control. "I didn't think being liked would matter to a man like you."

"'A man like me'?" he said tightly. It didn't matter. It shouldn't. Damn. Why did her approval suddenly matter at all? "Let me guess. You think I'm just buying another failing company to carve it up and sell it off at a profit, ruining lives and families in the process."

"Are you?"

"That's not what I do."

"No?"

Her scepticism ratcheted his annoyance up a notch. "I've saved more jobs than I've destroyed."

He shouldn't care. Hell, he didn't. But despite that, irritation flared and he suddenly leaned forward, making her jump. "I've publicly refuted every crooked claim, every accusation. But rebuttals don't sell papers—bad press does."

He tightened his jaw, refusing the fury access before pulling back with a disgusted snort. "Go on, name a story."

"I don't…"

"Do it, Holly. Name your damn price if that's what it'll take."

She inched back in her chair as far as she could go before saying quietly, "The East Timor construction company."

"The press said I bought it out and sacked the workers, leaving thousands of families without income. They glossed over the fact it was actually a front for a terrorist group. I dissolved the company and built a school in the local village instead."

They both paused as the waiter brought their food. But as the man left, Jake said curtly, "Next."

"I…"

"You want to know. I'm telling you." He forced his expression into neutrality, revealing nothing. "Next."

She swallowed and suddenly his eyes were drawn to her throat, to the heartbeat that was undoubtedly thumping wildly in her chest. "Paul Bradley."

"My chief financial officer." He picked up his fork, spearing the gnocchi with curt precision. "I demoted him to my Hanoi office because he vocally opposed one of my takeover bids."

Holly's fear suddenly gave way to anger, giving her the strength to face his stare with one of her own. "'Cross me and you'll pay'?"

"Yes. I demand loyalty in my staff. I won't stand any bad-mouthing, especially when he was wrong. I had to make an example of him."

"Was Mia Souris an example too?"

As a dark scowl creased his forehead, she blithely charged on. "She was your secretary and made a mint with her story. Why haven't you made her pay, too?"

"What makes you think she hasn't?"

At her sudden silence, he said softly, "The last I heard she was working as a waitress in a London club, trying to escape the notoriety of her kiss-and-tell article."

He placed his fork on the plate and drew the napkin slowly, almost sensuously, across his mouth. "You are a surprising woman, Holly McLeod."

"Why?" She studied her chicken penne, wondering how she'd manage to keep it down when her belly was churning so much.

"Are you pushing my buttons to get reassigned?"

Astonished, she jolted straight in her chair. "If you're unhappy about my performance, Mr Vance—"

"It's Jake, for Pete's sakes!" His voice then became less harsh. "Say it."

She said slowly, "Jake."

"Much better."

She blinked at the warm languor in his deep voice. "I just want to do my job."

He studied her for the longest time, until she began to wonder if she'd left a bit of food on her mouth or something.

"So let's just agree to focus on our jobs, shall we?" he said softly.

She nodded, suddenly desperate for space. With a low murmur, she excused herself and headed for the bathroom.

While Holly washed her hands at the sink, Jake's suggestion played over in her head. It made perfect sense. Do the job she'd been blackmailed into doing, get what she needed and move on.

If he was here for just an innocent pre-investment visit, then he'd have nothing to hide, right? But if his motives *were* ulterior, then for the sake of Blackstone's, she'd be justified in finding out what they were.

But as she straightened her skirt and rechecked her lipstick, she noticed her worried frown in the mirror. Quickly she smoothed it out. *Yeah, just keep telling yourself that, Holly.*

Jake watched Holly make a beeline for their table but before she could reach him, an impeccably dressed man intercepted her.

She whirled, and her look of surprise, then disgust, registered so clearly that Jake slowly stood. As the man whispered something then glanced over to Jake, her expression smoothed.

She sighed, shrugged and made her way back to the table.

With a frown, Jake remained standing, unashamedly taking advantage of his height against the shorter man. A man who was standing close to Holly. Too close for Jake's liking.

Irrational anger tightened his muscles, shocking the hell out of him. Through his surprise he heard Holly murmur, "Max, this is—"

"Jake Vance," Jake supplied and offered his hand.

Max smiled and returned the shake. "Max Carlton, head of Human Resources."

Ten seconds and Jake had him summed up. Immaculately groomed. Subtly cologned. Even without his intel, he could spot an office player a mile off. It was something in the eyes, the way they shifted and moved, the expression a concentrated effort in politeness. Carlton was too polished, too smooth, and his smile was a blokey smirk that Jake found offensive.

"So how's Holly working out for you, Jake?"

Jake noted Holly's frown. "Fine," he answered smoothly, as if their topic of conversation wasn't standing right next to him.

Max smiled, a man-to-man grin that set Jake's teeth on edge. "My assistant's one of a kind."

"Didn't she move to PR over a year ago?"

Max's face tightened and he glanced quickly at Holly, who gave him an innocent shrug.

"A temporary position," Max conceded stiffly. "If Holly's work performance makes the grade, there could possibly be a permanent transfer."

Jake was so intent on Max's visible unease that he almost missed Holly's start of surprise. Then, with a smooth adjustment to his tie, Max said, "If you've got any personnel or staffing questions, just give me a yell. Holly knows where to find me."

Under a rock, no doubt. Jake caught Max's wink at Holly, who ignored it with a dark frown. But when Carlton's gaze deliberately roamed down her neck to rest on the gentle curve of her breasts, his eyes narrowed. Intimate knowledge or wishful thinking? Either way it didn't stop a lick of fury from sparking in his belly.

Slowly he forced his fists to unclench.

"So…" Max said, tearing his eyes away, "I'd better be going. Nice to meet you, Jake."

Jake glared at Max's retreating back. He had no right to be angry. What Holly did or didn't do on her own time was not his business. She was Jake's assistant, for heaven's sakes, not his lover.

Pity.

Shaking off the jolt that felt like fire on his skin—especially in one particular part—he turned to Holly. "Charming guy."

"Some people think so. I just need his signature on my transfer."

"After you finish with me," he murmured, suddenly taken by the way her skin flushed underneath her cool mask of indifference.

She nodded and finally sat, checking her watch. "Yes. And you have thirty minutes."

"Thirty minutes for what?" He grinned, unable—or was that unwilling?—to keep the suggestiveness from his voice.

She blinked, clearly flustered. "Until your conference call with New York."

He gave her full points for maintaining that composure as they finished their meal in silence. But deep inside, on a purely predatory level, his mind registered the undeniable heat of desire.

Fool. It wasn't his mind that wanted Holly. It was something much more primal.

And what Jake Vance wanted, he usually got.

Four

Jake left his meeting with Kimberley Perrini with newfound respect. Despite his reluctance, Kim still pushed the idea of bringing Holly into their cone of silence. "She was the spin behind the Shipley University scandal, not to mention some of our internal issues. We're lucky to have her," Kim had said.

Grudgingly he had to agree. And if the press started running with pictures of him at Blackstone's, he knew exactly where to lay the blame.

Meanwhile, his security chief was busy compiling a list of enemies and disgruntled employees and their possible sources within Blackstone's. Matt Hammond had been suggested then discarded. No proof, plus the man got his fair share of negative press, too. Shareholders? No, too much to lose.

So he was back once again to a person Howard had personally offended.

And that's where it got confusing. Holly had had no direct contact with Howard. Blackstone's had put her through university. Outwardly, she was passionate about and dedicated to her job. She genuinely liked working here. Yet she was broke and floundering under a mountain of debt, and could still afford rent, food, clothes.

Was she that good an actress?

A shot of heat started low and crept up his body. Hazardous, thinking about Holly McLeod. Because if he did that, he'd have to acknowledge how paper-thin his control was. Instead of quenching his fire, his suspicion only stoked the flames higher, creating a burning need that was slowly dominating his every thought.

You have to stop thinking about her.

With a sharp snap, he opened the file in front of him and focused on Ryan's scrawling signature at the bottom of the page.

Jake leaned back in his chair. Underneath the stubbornness, the pride, he'd sensed Ryan's private pain. Only a close family member could hurt so deeply, scar so indelibly. Ryan refused to toe the line, said what he felt.

There's a lot of me in him.

Jake couldn't go back and change the past. God knows he would've tried years ago. He'd even admitted as much to Ryan. *I can't be angry at the woman who saved my life, who raised me as best she could. Who loved me. A lot of kids don't even get that.*

He'd hit an unexpected nerve with that, judging by the look on Ryan's face. And when he'd offered up the signed statutory declaration, formalizing his verbal promise to keep Blackstone's afloat, surprise had rendered Ryan speechless.

Jake sighed, suddenly tired of justifying something he

himself couldn't explain. Hell, there were a lot of things that would send his legal department into a spin if they only knew. For instance, last night he'd made a nice little profit on the NASDAQ, an event that would've normally brought him the usual adrenaline rush of satisfaction and pleasure. So how come it felt…less than a total rush?

He stood and stalked over to the small kitchenette in the corner of the office, tapping out his impatience as the coffee machine slowly dripped out the expensive Colombian blend.

Finally.

He grabbed the pot, pouring a cup that was one of many that day, forcing away his doubts with the first scalding sip.

You're doing the right thing, keeping a professional distance from the Blackstones. Getting emotionally involved can only mean disaster.

He'd fix Blackstone's, turn it around. That's what he did. He needed to seal this deal, to finish it, so he could get back to his life. A life that suddenly gaped wide, filled with hours of solitary existence.

He frowned and made his way over to the window, staring down at the Sydney CBD. It had changed over the years. He'd been an angry teenager alone in a huge concrete metropolis—a dangerous, exhilarating place for a small-town kid with something to prove. Over the years, through many major developments—some he himself had engineered—Sydney had grown and thrived. It was physical proof of his enormous success. Proof he was no longer the rebellious, stupid kid from the bush.

He sighed. He'd worked hard and long for all he had, steadily erasing that deep dark place in his heart, in his memory. He'd been doing fine until a week ago.

He turned away from the view as he rolled his neck. He needed a distraction. Yet when he glanced back at the financials on the desk, the paper blurred before his eyes. He needed something…warmer.

In the past, sex had taken the edge off, had enabled him to refocus and re-energise. And suddenly, all he could think about was a smart mouth and a kissy-mole.

He shoved his cup across the desk and coffee sloshed over the rim. With a low growl of frustration, he rubbed at the spreading stain.

Damn Blackstone's and its employees. He slouched into his chair and swivelled back to the window, searching for the familiar angles of AdVance Corp past the metallic curve of the Harbour Bridge, but when he found it, a stab of unfamiliar doubt hit him in the gut.

That's stupid. Amateur. Irrational. He'd made billions. He regularly dealt with Middle-Eastern kings and oil barons, dined with the cream of society, both here and overseas.

You're so far out of their league, you're off the planet.

He squeezed his eyes shut, so tight that silver spots danced behind his lids. There was no way those old fears were going to psyche him out.

They're Aussie royalty, and you're just the bastard son of an alcoholic mother.

Jake clenched his teeth and shoved those insidious doubts back with a vicious curse. His stepfather had chipped away at his self-esteem for years, always there with a comment, a sneer, a put-down when Jake screwed up. "You'll be in jail or dead by eighteen, boy," was his favourite line. He'd finally stood up to the son of a bitch a week before he'd left, leaving the man with a black eye and a broken hand. Since then, he'd been on his own, determined not to depend on anyone.

And now, suddenly, he had these people relying on him to make the right decision. To save their family legacy. A family that had been stolen from him thirty-two years ago.

Bitterness tightened his chest, the acrid tension weaving up his back to finally settle on his shoulders like a heavy cloak. He remembered too many towns, too many faces, taunting, teasing. April's sad expression, her face once so pretty and alive, suddenly weathered way beyond her fifty-four years. A woman filled with demons, her own personal and painful reasons for keeping a child from his rightful parents. He'd tried to escape his past, little knowing it wasn't his to escape from in the first place, even after every million he made, every deal he brokered, which earned him the respect and security he'd been craving.

"Ready for the grand tour?"

Momentarily disorientated, he snapped his eyes up to Holly standing in the doorway with the ever-present notepad and pen. For a few seconds he allowed himself to drink in her neat little figure, the curve of her cheek, the way her eyes steadily met his perusal. And as he did so, the vibrating bitterness gradually seeped out, leaving him suddenly empty and icy cold.

With a nod of finality, he shut those thoughts down and rose.

An excruciating hour later, Jake's normally tight control was in tatters. They'd gone through every floor in Blackstone's and he'd spent precisely sixty-two minutes in Holly's orbit, her gentle fragrance alternately arousing and frustrating him. Her soft, animated voice had tripped over his senses, aided traitorously by the memory of that kissy-mole when her mouth curved into a smile. When she walked, he'd ashamedly found his attention riveted to those curvy hips, swaying one tantalizing step ahead of him.

And her smell… He'd breathed in deeply, guiltily, more than once. Since when had a woman smelled so damn good?

The only time he'd not been thinking about touching her was when they'd passed Howard's trophy wall. Photos of the man opening the Blackstone's store. At some formal function. Shaking hands with the Prime Minister, the Queen, four U.S. past-presidents.

Jake had barely been able to contain a sneer. Howard had loved putting his stamp on everything he owned, flaunting his wealth and power. Like the way he'd displayed it on Ursula's neck.

Disgust bubbled up and with a scowl he choked it back down. He was not like Howard, despite Kimberley's assertion.

"Let's move on."

He jumped at Holly's soft intrusion, only to have his body react on a more primitive level when his eyes focused on her curves once again. The grey pinstriped skirt moulded her hips, emphasising a defined waist and womanly hips. Her shirt was bright blue, making her eyes stand out, the elbow-length sleeves showing off long arms with a watch on one wrist, a simple gold bangle on the other.

Absently he'd wondered if she had on any makeup at all, given how fresh her face looked. How touchable it looked.

He shoved his hands deep into his pockets and nodded. He imagined Holly taking the news about his real identity with outward calm, a facade that covered up the fact she was a deep thinker. He'd noticed more than once the realities of her thoughts clearly mirrored in her expressive blue eyes.

No, not blue, more green. Like the complexity of shades in the deep ocean, where the—

His thoughts screeched to a halt. Since when had he obsessed about a woman's eyes before?

Yet despite his control, an unwanted ache started in his groin. An ache that couldn't be ignored when, an hour after the tour was over, Jake shoved his way into Blackstone's executive gym.

Instead of solitude, a stretching Holly on the treadmill confronted him, scattering all thoughts of a long hard run to clear his mind.

He stared. And stared. In short bike pants and a cropped sports top, she was gripping one tanned muscular leg behind her in a quad stretch, the white Lycra pulling tight across her breasts as they rose with her deep breaths. As his mouth went dry, she rolled her shoulders and her long ponytail dragged over her damp skin.

Her breath sighed out, quickly engulfing his brain, the part that was still functioning.

His bag dropped unheeded to the floor. She kept right on stretching, her shoulder blades flexing and contracting with the effort.

Swish of the hair.

Deep sigh.

He groaned, ready to beat a hasty retreat, but she must have sensed him because she whirled, pulling out her earbuds. She quickly dropped her leg and grabbed her towel, her chest rising as a trickle of sweat ran down her throat and disappeared in the cleft beneath her damp tank. He followed that journey, until he reluctantly dragged his eyes back up to meet hers.

"Leaving?" he murmured.

"Yes." In record time, she pulled a sweatshirt over her head then scooped up her bag, quickly heading for the door.

He just stood there, the air as she hightailed it past him yawning cold and empty. Then he heard the door click with finality.

As the gym doors closed behind her, Holly wrapped her arms around her body to ward off the chill. *Escape first, then put on your track pants.* She thought she'd nearly succeeded until Jake appeared beside her.

"Yours," he said gruffly, holding out her iPod. She paused, glanced at his hand, then up at his face. A blank, stern face devoid of all warmth.

She slowly took her iPod and couldn't help but notice he relinquished it without making skin contact. "Thanks." She turned back to the elevator, repositioned her bag on her shoulder and stared at the ascending floor numbers.

When he remained still, she shot a quick look in his direction. "Working late?"

"This is early for me."

She smiled thinly but said nothing.

"But…?" he prompted.

"Don't you ever take a day off?"

He shrugged. "Too much work to do."

"What's the point of making all that money if you can't enjoy yourself?"

He frowned. "I'm not unhappy with what I've achieved, Holly. Money doesn't make you miserable."

"No. People do that all by themselves." The elevator doors swung open, signalling the end to their strange conversation. But to Holly's surprise he followed her in. The doors swished closed and in the next second, he pushed the stop button.

"And to answer your question, I enjoy myself plenty."

She stilled, her breath rattling around, too harsh in her throat, her heart beating too loudly in her chest. She looked at him, noting his narrowed eyes, the sudden tension in his body as it practically sizzled…not with anger but something else, something indefinable that he struggled to contain.

Apprehension chugged through her body, leaving her immobile. Wasn't he supposed to be ice cold in the face of adversity?

Then he fixed on her mouth and she felt a hot flush start in her belly and fan upwards. She parted her lips, the air in her lungs thickly seeping out. Was he actually thinking about kissing her?

He moved quickly, so smoothly for a man the size of Ayers Rock that it took the rest of her breath away. Or maybe it was the kiss stealing all her will to function properly. It froze her limbs, stuttered her heartbeat. Erased all the memories of other kisses that had come before.

When his hot mouth covered hers in deep possession, his hands buried in her hair, preventing escape, a low groan escaped her. The kiss, the sheer power and force of it, stole her will, along with any denials she may have entertained. All that existed was Jake and the force of his kiss, the utter command of his lips sliding over hers and his tongue invading her mouth.

She took a deep, shuddering breath as her eyes fluttered closed. His smell was so different from anything she'd experienced, the heat, the passion. When his hands cupped her face, holding her in place, Holly kissed him right back.

* * *

It did Jake in, finally having her lush mouth beneath his, that tiny mole teasing the corner, his to kiss. The mole that had distracted him time and again for hours on end.

Her skin scorched him, as if a furnace burned just below the surface. Suddenly the desire to have her naked, to be against the rest of that silken skin, crashed into him.

His hands were under her sweatshirt and he hit what he was seeking—hot, damp flesh. But like an addict craving more, he wasn't satisfied with the mere touch of her skin, the feel of her rib cage under his questing hand. He wanted—needed—more.

With his blood pounding thickly in his veins, the ache in his groin an almost unbearable tightness, he found the edge of her tank top and eased his way under to the gentle curve of one breast.

Her sudden gasp snapped him back to reality, and he wrenched his mouth away from the temptation of hers.

What the hell are you doing?

From a great gaping distance he heard Holly's breathless question, thick with passion.

"Jake?"

She'd never know how difficult it was to withdraw from the pleasures her body promised. How much he ached to succumb to the raging passion that forced beads of sweat to run down his back.

Desire grabbed at him, yanked and twisted his brain until he was left hot, hard and frustrated. But with a shuddering sigh, he withdrew and stepped back, the cool air rushing into the gaping chasm between their bodies.

"Pull your shirt down," he said, knowing it came out more

harshly than he intended when the light of desire flickered and died on Holly's face.

Self-disgust filled him, quickly followed by guilt. He'd lost control. For the first time in years he'd lost it.

He wanted to reach out to her, offer some kind of apology, but if her crossed arms and steely back were any indication, he'd have a better chance of flying to the moon.

Slowly, he released the emergency stop button and with a sudden jerk, the elevator started up. "I'll take you home."

She shot him an incredulous look. "I'm not your responsibility, Jake. I can catch a cab."

"Look," he said slowly, turning to her. "We…"

"Jake, I understand." She refused to meet his eyes as the elevator doors slid open. "It's not a big deal."

Jake stared at her retreating back, the words stuck to the roof of his mouth. Not a big deal? So how come he suddenly felt the urgency to taste her right now? To have those shapely legs wrap around his waist and feel the erotic glide as he buried himself deep inside her?

Dammit. Now he was hard again.

With a soft curse, he pressed the basement button before he did something even more foolish than what he'd just already done.

As the morning sun crept cautiously into her bedroom, Holly lay staring at the ceiling. What on earth had possessed her to kiss Jake Vance? The implication sent a wave of cold reality over her hot skin. They'd been about to… She shook her head. And how she had wanted to. Still wanted to.

It shouldn't be. He stood for everything she despised, everything that had taken away her family and forced her into his spying role. But when she tried summoning up righteous anger all that emerged was an overwhelming mesh of confusion. It happened every time he glanced her way, ran that frankly sensual gaze over her face, let it linger on her mouth.

Despite her best efforts, she was acutely interested in him. How could she be so attracted if he was truly the bad guy everyone was intent on perpetuating?

You're an intelligent woman, Holly McLeod. Apart from one obvious glitch, you can tell the good guys from the bad. Yet Jake was a study in extremes. Corporate raider or saviour? Genuine attraction or predatory lust? He'd gotten her so wound up she didn't know what to believe any more.

Deep in thought, she walked slowly into the bathroom, and by the time she'd fixed her makeup and left for work, her bad mood had been replaced by the day's schedule.

She walked into Blackstone's foyer with a sigh of relief. With coffee in one hand, handbag in the other, she'd survived the early morning bustle of George Street and a sharp biting wind that had determinedly yanked at her coattails. But after she pushed the elevator button and the doors opened, her luck ran out.

Jake Vance. In the flesh. In the warm, heated, taut flesh that she knew felt, smelled, tasted divine.

"Good morning, Holly."

The warm intimacy of his voice, combined with the small interior swamped her, leaving goose bumps on her skin.

"Good morning." She repositioned her cappuccino while hitching her bag on her shoulder.

As the elevator sped smoothly upwards, she surreptitiously eyed him. Twice she started to say something, and twice she hesitated, swallowing the words on the tip of her tongue. Surely he'd say something about last night, even just to set her straight with a familiar *It didn't mean anything. Let's just keep things professional.*

Yet he remained silent, reading his newspaper in complete and utter concentration. As she stared at his firm grip on the pages, her brain flashed back to last night, to this same place, to those long skilful fingers. The way they'd teased. The way he'd touched her as his tongue had eased inside her mouth.

She swallowed a shocked gasp, snapping her focus back to the doors.

"Do you have anything specific on the agenda today?" She forced cool professionalism into her voice. Unfortunately, her idea of broaching a business-related topic only effectively made her the center of his attention.

His slow perusal of her was thorough and hot. She tried to ignore it but on every level, her body tingled with the attention. Instead she determinedly stared at the ascending numbers. *Surely if you don't look at him, he'll lose his effect. Like a solar eclipse.*

"I have meetings," he said. "Look, Holly. About last night."

And here it comes. Holly shook her head, hot embarrassment flooding her cheeks as the doors slid open. Quickly she strode out, escaping the warm intimacy that reminded her of last night. He followed closely. "You don't need to—"

"It was—"

The both paused awkwardly as Holly unlocked the glass door until she blurted out, "It doesn't matter. Really."

His eyes narrowed, darkening. "Doesn't it?" he challenged. "I think it matters more than you want to admit."

"How would you know?" She tried for nonchalance as she walked in and placed her coffee carefully on the desk.

"Because I know how to read people. You were an eager participant in that kiss."

She flushed. "Is that how you win—by figuring out what people want then turning it against them?"

"I present them with an offer they can't refuse."

On another man, the arrogance would have forced a sharp, scornful rebuttal from her lips. On Jake, there was no egotism or conceit. It was simply a statement of truth.

She tipped her head. "So there's nothing you've wanted that you couldn't have."

Danger. She sensed it the very moment Jake's eyes darkened. The air seemed to thicken, and the seconds ticked by on the clock so loudly they echoed the beat of her heart as it upped tempo.

"I still have…things I want to achieve."

She finally dragged her eyes away, unable to bear the intensity in his any longer. It was like a promise, a weird prediction of the future, of her and him together. Completely.

"What about a wife? A child to leave all your wealth to?"

"Eventually." A stab of emotion, totally unexpected, tightened his jaw for one brief second. Then he blinked and his signature expression of cool blankness took over.

So he had thought about that. And letting her know irritated him, for some reason. Why? Did he view it as some kind of weakness? Or… She swallowed a small guilty breath. Did Mia's betrayal still affect the unfeeling Mr Midas Touch?

After he closed his office door, Holly suddenly realised they'd both avoided discussing the implications of last night. And that non-closure worried her.

Five

Any normal girl would be out on a date Saturday night, Holly muttered to herself as she walked into Blackstone's, bravado propelling her forward. Not at work, spying on her boss. Not sneaking around, trying to uncover Jake's big plot to bring down Blackstone's.

As the elevator sped up to the top floor, Holly recalled the past hour. Kimberley had offered her two tickets to the Alex Perry fashion show at the Powerhouse Museum as compensation for pulling her from the preparations. Sitting through the traditional bridal theme closing with gorgeous women strutting about in stunning white gowns wasn't exactly what Holly had in mind to occupy her thoughts. Then she'd spotted Jake in the front row and her evening had suddenly ratcheted up in the interesting column.

He was seated next to one of Blackstone's prominent shareholders, engaged in deep conversation, when some sixth sense must have told him he was being watched. He glanced up and pinned her with his dark gaze.

Her clothes had suddenly felt constrictive. She may as well have been naked sitting there, the off-the-shoulder wrap-around designer blouse providing absolutely no coverage whatsoever.

He had no right to stare at her like that. And less right to make her feel…hot. Bothered.

Aroused.

She rose quickly, murmured something about fresh air to Miko, her surprised flatmate, and made her way to the exit. Strobe lights flashed behind her, loud music throbbed low and sensual, but she kept right on walking—even when she realised that Jake had a perfect view of her backside clad in skintight black velvet hipsters. Another brilliant decision gone horribly wrong.

She was waiting in line at the open-air bar, eyeing the congregation of smokers on her left, when a man broke free from the group and strode over.

Max.

A wave of cigarette smoke reached her before he did and burnt her nostrils. She barely suppressed a cough of distaste as he crossed his arms on the bar next to her, bumping his shoulder into hers.

"What are you doing here?" she said and angled away.

"Socializing. Having a few drinks. Keeping an eye on you. You've been avoiding me."

Ignoring his oh-so-charming smirk, she reached for her glass but quickly recoiled when Max reached it first.

He frowned. "Holls, don't be like that."

She just scowled and pulled the glass back, wine slopping over the rim as she resisted the overwhelming desire to clock him with it.

"Jake's getting to you, huh?"

She gritted her teeth, praying for control. "Haven't you got someone else to blackmail, Max?"

Max laughed an unpleasant bark. "Watch it, Holls. It's not just me who's got something to lose here."

"*You* were the one sleeping around. *You* were the one who offered me up as Jake's assistant. And you—"

"And you were the one who didn't say no to sex on my desk. We had a good time, Holly. Admit it—you got off on the whole 'secret and forbidden' thing."

Disbelief rendered her speechless. She didn't know what was worse, her raging stupidity for ignoring Blackstone's morality clause, or her naivety for thinking she'd be any different from the rest of Max's women.

It was those innocent choirboy looks, complete with a mop of golden curls that made Max Carlton such a hit. The men liked him for his after-hours drinks and blokey talk about football and women. The women were flattered by his charm and good looks. And to her surprise, there'd been a spark of interest despite the unofficial gossip. He was an attractive smooth-talker and everyone knew it, especially Max Carlton.

So you fell for it and now he's got you over a barrel. Way to go, Holly.

"What do you want?" Before she could blink, he took her arm and steered her across the courtyard to a dark corner.

She wrenched from his grip, her breath coming quick and angry. Thank goodness for public places. Past him, she noticed the caterer's tables, the half-dozen people setting up for the hungry masses.

"What have you found out?"

"Nothing," she said, disgust clogging her voice. "Jake Vance is above board on this one."

Max smiled thinly. "We're talking about the same guy, right? Men like Vance don't just waltz into a company with good intentions. They destroy them."

"He's not here for a takeover. And I'm sure Ric or Ryan would have—"

Max snorted. "They're too busy playing happy families. Vance has 'em fooled. Listen." He stepped closer, an intimidating figure in the half-shadows. "I've got a good thing going at Blackstone's and I plan to keep it that way. Just get me proof of Vance's intentions. After I get compensated by the board—"

"You'll sign off on my permanent PR transfer."

"Yeah, sure." He reached out to touch her cheek but she flinched. He narrowed his eyes. "Make no mistake, Holly. If you blab, I'll take you down with me. Whom do you think the board will believe?"

Then he swiftly tipped the glass of wine down her shirt. Holly choked off a squeal and jumped back, too late. The dark wet stain spread rapidly over the chiffon, dripping down her front.

Max looked nonplussed. "Jake's busy chatting up the models. Go back to the office and change. And check out his desk."

The elevators pinged open, startling Holly into the present. The insides of her mouth were arid and scratchy. It was all about Max—his job, his comfort. No thought as to how this corporate espionage went against every decent bone in her body.

She tamped a lid on her emotions. Panic had never solved her problems before; it wouldn't now.

Slowly she walked out, unlocked the glass doors then closed them behind. She'd worked late and on the weekends before, which meant the security guy had suspected nothing amiss. She'd strode into the building with her head held high, even tossing him a wave as she walked over to the executive elevator. But now, standing stock still inside the darkened office, trepidation fluttered in her belly.

"Just get changed and leave," she muttered to herself. "You can stall Max another couple of days."

Bolstered, she turned on the desk lamp and laid her key card on the filing cabinet. She checked the hallway then plucked a shirt from her locker and swung open Jake's office door.

She changed in the shadows, and just as quickly, she scanned his desk. The brochures she'd finally managed to give him lay open on the top. She glanced at the financials in his in tray.

No. You can't.

Yet what could she do? It was either help Max or get fired. Despite her desperate need for the money, she genuinely loved working here. She'd carved a niche, made friends and garnered the respect of her colleagues. She prided herself on working hard and being professional, and Kimberley, for one, had noticed that.

So professional you breached your employment contract and had sex with your boss.

She swallowed, fighting with nerves until finally she made a decision. With a determined slant to her mouth, she strode around the desk and tried the drawers. Locked. She shuffled through the papers, flicked open the folders but came up empty-handed.

Holly paused, her mind buzzing. Or perhaps it was the

subtle hint of cologne, all male and all Jake, invading her senses that sent a shock of remembrance through her brain.

Jake's mouth, warm and needy on hers.

Her breath shook on the way in. She stilled, listening in the stillness to the guilty beating of her heart.

It was then that two things caught her attention: a tiny green light coming from the phone recharger on the edge of his desk. And the soft swoosh of the glass door opening in the outer office. He'd come back for his mobile phone.

Panic clogged her throat. *Think, think!* With a held breath she quickly stepped from behind the desk and undid the buttons on her blue silk shirt. It hung open, showing a glimpse of her black satin bra, when Jake opened his office door.

She didn't have to fake a gasp as he swung the door wide. When he zeroed right in on her cleavage, she breathed a sigh of relief. Her smokescreen had worked.

"I spilled wine on my shirt," she hurried to explain. Yet when his eyes dragged over her skin, leaving it practically sizzling in his wake, she self-consciously tugged at the shirt-front, realising the danger of her situation.

His hand stilled on the door handle. Light spilled around the frame, silhouetting his body in stark relief. To her chagrin the shadows also hid his expression. It didn't hide the deep timbre in his soft statement, however.

"Really."

She gestured to the windows covered with blinds. "Your office has coverage. I had a spare shirt in my locker…." She began buttoning it up, suddenly feeling stupid and exposed.

"You left the closing show early?" she asked unnecessarily.

"So did you."

He moved, walking into the small pool of light from the

desk lamp. Shadows slashed across his face, illuminating the darkness and light of his features. An elegantly straight nose. The dark hooded brows. The angular cheekbones combined with a strong, almost glacial jawline.

"Are you really here to change your shirt, Holly?"

"I…I…" *Think, Holly!* Yes? No? Arrghh. Seeing her hope fading gradually away, she leaned back, bumping her bottom on the desk. That small movement commanded Jake's eyes back to her open neckline, lingering. As his eyes dipped into a frown, she caught something else in their depths. Desire.

She held her breath as the room spun.

He drew out the words softly when he spoke. "What are you doing, Holly?"

"I…" Panic had rendered her voice husky, and she cleared her throat before adding lamely, "My shirt."

She tried a smile on for size, one that faltered when he remained silent. *Oh, for heaven's sake!* She drew herself up with all the courage she could muster, fully prepared to walk out if only her legs weren't about to buckle under the weight of her trembling body. She even started forward, getting to within a metre of freedom, but instead of standing aside he remained rooted to the spot, a huge immovable mountain of brooding male.

"Excuse me." She stepped to the side, attempting to boldly brush past. That proved to be her first mistake.

He grabbed her arm, stilling her departure. She opened her mouth to protest but, in doing so, glared up at him. Her second and fatal mistake.

His green gaze blazed down at her like a newly stoked fire, the muscles on his face tightening, his jaw straining with effort.

Retreat proved an impossibility. She'd irrevocably invaded

his comfort zone. Her blood buzzed as he stood there, ramrod straight, her arm firmly in his grip. Her skin burned from the contact, the silk no barrier for his scorching heat. Undeniable tension unfurled from his body as their eyes clashed, warring like two familiar adversaries. He shifted and Holly held her breath. Was he going to…?

When he gave a ragged sigh and abruptly let her go, turning away to shove a hand through his hair, she muffled a small moan of perverse disappointment. She didn't realise he'd heard it until his taut body stilled.

It was as if everything was caught in a freeze frame. The tension in the air practically crackled.

She knew the exact moment he crossed the unspoken line between chaos and control because everything happened all at once. Suddenly. Unexpectedly. With an oath he whirled and crushed her in a deep, punishing kiss.

He ground his mouth into hers, demanding acquiescence, and amazingly, she gave it to him. Heaven help her, she wanted this. Their tongues tangled as a fierce and frenzied passion swelled up inside her. With her damp body plastered to his, his heat quickly soaked through her shirt, sparking off a desperate desire to have him inside her, here and now.

He was made for pleasuring a woman, she realised dazedly as his mouth moved down to her neck and sucked gently. Every touch, every hot breath elicited her abandoned response—a groan, a gasp, a sigh. He approached the task of pleasing her with complete and utter focus, every move determined and skilled. Unlike other men, he seemed finely attuned to her body, knew exactly what to do to have her trembling.

Through a red-hot daze, Holly felt cool air on her body and realised her shirt was on the floor. Before she could take a breath, he'd backed her up against the cold glass door. Freezing glass on her back, hot Jake at the front. Hot and cold. Just like the man himself. So intensely passionate yet so cool in the boardroom. His expression was a study in tight control as he hoisted her legs up and wrapped them around his waist.

They spent long, aching minutes like that, Jake supporting her weight as he took his time to feast on her, placing scorching kisses along her neck before returning to her mouth. When she thought she'd pass out from pleasure, he grasped her bottom and turned, easing her onto the edge of his desk.

Passion nipped at Jake's self-control as he dragged his hands down her back, over the curve of her sweet butt that had teased him with her fashion-show exit. The velvet rubbed erotically against his palms and he pulled her against his throbbing groin, pinning her to the spot. She offered a muffled groan against his mouth and kept right on kissing him.

Heat exploded, consuming his body in a flaming inferno as he eased his fingers under the waistband of her pants. With her hips thrust forward, he bent her back over the desk, palming her stomach as their mouths and tongues tangled in damp seduction.

Papers scattered to the floor, followed by the thump of a file. She propped her elbows on the desk, bracing herself, which allowed him to ease his knee between her legs.

She felt so good. Tasted even better. But he wanted more.

He quickly found her zipper and in a nanosecond, his hand dived in to cup the warm curls between her legs.

She gasped beneath him and for one gut-wrenching second, he thought she'd balk. Amazingly, though, she parted her legs and drew him down for another kiss.

Color burst behind his eyelids as he let out a shuddering

groan. In one determined movement he slipped his finger into her wet, hot core, and with that, his world shattered in a thousand pieces.

Holly was consumed by scorching heat, every one of her cautious warnings reduced to ashes beneath his masterful hands. Her breasts throbbed as they slid against his chest, a wall of hot, tempered steel beneath his sinfully luxurious shirt. His tiepin rubbed against her bra, creating an erotically painful friction that pebbled her nipples. And below that incredible sensation came another—the intimate stroking of his finger, buried deep inside her.

Oh, my.

His mouth left hers, leaving a hot trail of wet kisses from her sensitive collarbone before finally coming to rest on her breast. There, he tongued her nipple through the bra, teasing it, while with one slow deliberate movement, he eased another finger into her.

It took all of Jake's self-control to pause right there, to feel the deep pulse of her muscles surrounding him, to hear the soft mewling coming from her lush mouth and not completely lose it. Ferocious desire scorched every vein, every nerve ending of his body. His groin was harder than granite, straining against his pants, desperate to bury inside her. Meanwhile, blood thundered in his brain, blocking all rational thought. A thick groan welled up in his throat as he clawed for control.

Beyond the sound of his harsh, ragged breath came her soft gasps. "Jake, please…"

She squirmed under him frantically, clenching her muscles around his fingers. He squeezed his eyes shut, commanding his body to remain in control, even as his groin throbbed hard and hot.

"Jake!"

Her plea undid him and with a curse and a prayer, he continued, plunging deep into her wetness then easing out slowly as she hissed in pleasure. He gritted his teeth, trying to block out her deep sighs of satisfaction, the way her lips moved over his, nibbling, wanting. *I can't...can't...*

And then she gasped. Her whole body stilled in tense, expectant pleasure. He watched her eyes widen, pupils dilate with arousal, her mouth round in a shocked little *oh*.

Knowing she was powerless to stop the hot waves of release crash over her, Holly shuddered. She clung to him, feeling her heartbeat thunder away in her chest, matching the heavy thud of his as she pressed her face to his chest.

Soon, too soon, her breath slowed, yet still he held her. She allowed herself the fantasy, squeezing her eyes shut and deliberately forcing her doubts back from the edges of reality.

But eventually she felt his hands pressing gently on her shoulders, his tension straining as he withdrew. Was it regret tempering every ounce of his body as he stepped back and turned away? Cold air rushed her skin, bringing clarity to her thoughts. *What the hell had she done?*

"I'll take you home," he finally said, his back to her.

"You don't have to."

He didn't look at her, just remained a silhouette, his jaw clenched in the dim light. "I do. Get dressed."

His soft command landed like a cold slap of reality on her hot cheek. She struggled with her shirt, embarrassment flushing her neck. If that weren't enough, she realised that she'd have to face him Monday. And the next day, and the next. Instead of a spy, he probably just thought she was unprofessional and easy.

That thought made her want to throw up.

The ride was mercifully quick, considering it was close to one in the morning and the whole of Sydney seemed to be on the road.

The car stopped and Jake glanced over at her. Her eyes looked glassy and tired. He shook his head. Sobering up, most likely.

He led her to the door, let her fumble in her purse for her keys. When she swung it open, he followed her inside.

"Thanks," she mumbled politely, and headed straight down the slate-floor hallway.

He watched the gentle sway of her hips for agonizing seconds, mesmerised by the way the velvet cupped the rounded cheeks of her butt. With his groin still throbbing, he whirled and forced himself to focus on his surroundings.

The living area was to his right, a large L-shaped space with a huge wide-screen TV and accompanying electronic gadgets. A dark blue corner couch sat against the wall, while a few side tables, a display wall of books, photos and awards filled the space.

He walked in, picked up a trophy and eyed the inscription. *Miko Tarasai—2007 Sydney University Netball Championships.*

She had a flatmate.

He turned and cast an eye over the photos—shots of a Chinese family against the backdrop of Hong Kong. The same young girl with a Labrador. A very young Holly and an old couple—her parents, judging by the similarities—posing in Akubras and leaning against an old gum tree.

Jake turned and walked down the hall. In the dimly lit kitchen he saw Holly open the fridge and search around inside.

"You own this place?"

She jumped at the sound of his voice. "Don't you know that already?"

"No." He waited for her to emerge but, after a few seconds, said softly, "Are you going to freeze to death to avoid looking at me?"

With an aggrieved sigh, she slammed the fridge closed, a half-empty bottle of something dark and red in her hand.

"Don't you think you've had enough?"

She scowled. "It's grape juice. Please go home."

"Not until I know you're OK."

With a sarcastic slant to her mouth, she held out her arms then pirouetted. "See? I'm in one piece. Now leave."

"Holly, we should talk about what happened." He hesitated and as he watched her, the flush on her cheeks began to grow.

"You don't need to say anything."

"It was just something that—"

"—happened," she finished for him.

"Yeah." *Something incredibly hot.*

"We're two professional people. It was a…" She faltered as his scowl deepened. "A lapse in judgement. Let's concentrate on our jobs and forget this happened, OK?"

Forget a tornado hadn't just swept into his life and turned it upside down? Jake wanted to interject, but the expression on her face was nine-parts resolve, one-part vulnerability. She needed him to agree.

"I'm hoping I can rely on your discretion," she continued, confirming his suspicions. "And I hope you won't tell the Blackstones about this. I signed a morality clause and—"

"I'm not your boss."

She blinked. "Technically, no. But Legal could interpret it differently."

If her look of apprehension hadn't swayed him, the gentle beseeching in her eyes did. He'd never had a woman plead with him before over something so innocent.

Right. There was nothing innocent about what they'd done, what they would've done. What he really wanted to do.

He felt his body stir again and cursed himself long and hard.

"You have my word," he said with a nod.

As if she'd been holding her breath, the tension in her body flooded out. And when she gave him a grateful smile, he watched her little kissy-mole move with the curve of her lips.

He muffled a groan. It was a smile that was all about thanking him, not turning him on, yet amazingly it achieved both. It flared in his memory, reminding him how she'd felt beneath his mouth, surrounding his fingers.

"Well, it's late," Holly said lamely. Something had changed, something dark and hot in the dim light of her kitchen as she shifted her weight from foot to foot, willing him to go. Yet her mother had taught her to be polite, so like a good-mannered girl, she waited for Jake to be true to character and leave.

He didn't.

A breeze sprang up, carrying with it a tinkling sound from the balcony. He glanced across to the closed doors. "Wind chimes?"

She said slowly, "Yes. My flat mate is Chinese. She's into feng shui."

"She decorated the flat."

"No, actually I did. She just approved the final colors and furnishings. It's her parents' place."

"You have an eye for color."

"I wanted to be an interior designer, but—" She paused. *You want him to leave, not engage him in further conversation.*

"Couldn't afford the risk?" he said casually.

"You know I couldn't. I needed a steady job."

Instead of rising to that, he pulled the sliding glass doors open an inch, letting the cool wind blow in.

She sighed. "Are you staying to discuss my decorating skills?"

"Maybe I just like your company."

She drew in a sharp breath. "Are you enjoying this?"

"Enjoying what?" He cast an eye over the rolling dark clouds outside, then back to her.

"This…uncomfortable moment."

"Is that what it is?" he murmured. "Just 'uncomfortable'?"

She drew back, painting an invisible barrier around herself. "It's late. Good night, Jake."

The scowl bloomed across his face, confusing her. But before she could even try to interpret that, he nodded. "Good night."

One second he was there, the next he was gone. After she heard the door click, the tension in her limbs rushed out like air from a balloon. With a soft groan, she dragged herself over to the balcony, slumped into the patio chair and drew her knees up, allowing herself to wallow in the moment of self-pity.

Why couldn't she ever learn from her mistakes? First Max, now Jake. How foolish could one woman be when it came to matters of the heart? She'd not only put her job in jeopardy again with a stupid lapse in judgement, but she'd also failed Max's ultimatum.

One second, then two and she breathed deep. No way would she let this beat her…let Max beat her. On Monday she'd confess Max's blackmail to Kimberley, plead her innocence and throw herself at her mercy. On Monday she'd be strong and face her mistakes head-on.

And what of Jake? Was that a mistake too?

She allowed herself a brief memory—the searing heat of his mouth, the exquisite torture of his hands, the burning desire in his eyes.

She swallowed, her throat as dry as parchment. How much would he want her if he knew the truth?

Six

Kimberley Perrini arrived ten minutes early on Monday for her emergency meeting with Jake, taking a seat at the small conference table in his office. Holly had always admired Kim for her forthrightness, her resilience and the poise she'd retained in the face of the whole Blackstone's scandal these past few months. As usual, she was impeccable in a dark green business shirt and long, tailored skirt, despite the touch of worry in her eyes.

"Jake isn't running you too ragged, I hope?" she inquired.

Ragged? Holly's pulse hitched. "No."

"The man is quite…" Kim trailed off, looking thoughtful "…intense."

Holly merely nodded, not trusting herself to speak. Thanks to last night, she knew more about him than she'd thought possible. Intimate things.

It was bad enough trying to maintain a professional workplace without letting Saturday night take over her brain. He'd invaded her dreams, hot, erotic ones that forced her awake in a tangle of sheets and a throbbing between her legs.

"This assignment won't be for much longer," Kim was saying. "We miss you in PR."

"I miss it too." Holly rose, retrieving a document from the printer while trying to squelch her thoughts. "Listen, I need to talk to you about something…" She trailed off as Jake, then Ric Perrini, walked in the door.

"Later, OK?" Kim was already turning away and Holly could do nothing but nod.

As Jake strode past with a murmured greeting, her body betrayed her. Her heart began to pound and her skin tingled. She glanced away, only to catch the intimate look passing between Ric and Kim, followed by a small smile on Kim's lips and the answering gleam in her husband's eyes.

They were in love. Despite their tumultuous past, they were deeply, head over heels in love. Holly barely had time to swallow her envy before Ryan strode in, shattering the moment.

"Have you seen this?" Ryan shoved the financial section onto the conference table as Garth entered and closed the door. The heading Takeover At Blackstone's? blared out in bold type.

Jake shrugged. "The shares are stable."

"For now," Ryan replied, unconvinced.

"So some people have seen me about. It was bound to happen. We all know it's no more true than Briana Out, Mystery Woman In."

Holly flushed as all eyes turned to her. With his ex Briana Davenport, taken by Jarrod Hammond, did the press think *she* was Briana's replacement? She glanced at Jake, whose mouth was curved in irony. Unable to look away, she focused on those lips for seconds longer than necessary.

Lips that she had imagined last night, kissing her in places she'd never think could react to such soft contact. Expert lips, warm and welcoming and completely open to taking their kiss further. Dangerous lips. Dangerous fingers.

Focus!

"Who? W-where?" she said, stammering.

"Us, in some gossip magazine. Seems we now have a personal relationship. First diamond shopping, then lunch. Who knows where it may lead. Perhaps an office liaison?"

He was mocking her. That green-eyed devil was actually mocking her!

"Which is a good lead-in to this meeting," Kim said smoothly, turning to Holly as they were all seated. "We've recently found out and proved that Jake is actually our missing brother, James Blackstone. We've also agreed you need to know the truth behind Jake's presence at Blackstones."

Holly hesitated for a heartbeat, filling the silence with a slow intake of breath. "I'm sorry, did you say—?"

"Yes," Jake interjected calmly.

She felt her mouth sag but recovered quickly, snapping it shut so hard she felt her teeth click. Stunned, she looked from Kim back to Jake, only to come up against a familiar brick wall. She took a deep breath to calm herself.

"You're really James Blackstone?" she said on a breath.

Man, did Max have it wrong. Now things made complete sense—why Jake wanted to know about the company, the nagging familiarity in his emerald eyes, so like Kim's and Ryan's. And why, even as Jake Vance, that irrefutable Blackstone aura of entitlement and power shone through.

There was so much she needed to ask. But as she floundered, gathering her thoughts, Kim said, "I don't need to tell you we're expecting the utmost confidence on this issue, Holly."

Holly nodded mutely, firmly suppressing her curiosity. "Of course." Nonetheless, her eyes still made a beeline for Jake, who was watching her with an intensity she found acutely disturbing.

"Everyone tells me you're an expert in spin," Jake said now, his eyebrows raised questioningly.

"Well, I…" She forced her voice to steady. "There've been no complaints."

Kim said, "At my request, Holly's prepared something we're sure will combat the negative press."

Holly breathed in, focusing on the presentation in front of her. With a confident flick, she opened it. "A charity ball with a combined auction." She surveyed the Blackstones, who sat silent and thoughtful. "We approach retailers for donations— a romantic cruise, Blackstone jewellery, a weekend retreat, gift packs, LCD TVs, that sort of thing—then the guests bid on them. I drafted a press release," she said, pushing a page over to Jake. "I also thought we could explain Mr Vance… uh…Blackstone—"

"Vance," said Jake calmly, taking pity on her.

She flushed. "—Mr Vance's presence by auctioning off a two-week apprenticeship at AdVance Corp."

"Which means what, exactly?" Jake said.

"The highest bidder gets to be your apprentice for two weeks, accompanying you to meetings and learning the ins and outs of business from your unique perspective."

His smile was sceptical. "And you think people will bid on this?"

"Of course. My other idea is a bachelor auction—"

"No."

She stopped and, in the silence, handed out her proposal to everyone. Finally Garth said, "What about preparation time?"

"We've organised other events in less," Holly said. "We'll use the Grand Ballroom downstairs, of course. Kim and I agreed on the last Saturday night in May."

Garth looked thoughtful. "That's under three weeks away. You'd need to get the announcement out tomorrow, especially in light of today's paper."

Kim added, "We'll time our publicity push to generate positive spin leading up to the ball."

"But what of the bigger problem?" Garth fixed Jake with a steely look. "I've been talking discreetly with our shareholders and the message is the same. As a family company with long-standing investors, Jake's business reputation is not the only thing that worries them."

"I can't help that," Jake interjected.

"Ahh, but you can. That construction company takeover you brokered last week didn't help, especially when their chief accountant jumped from the window."

"It was the second floor. He lived," Jake said calmly, ignoring Holly's gasp. "And the man was being charged with bribing a local politician."

"But my point is—"

"Your point means curtailing my business transactions. No."

Everyone paused, letting that sink in until Ric said, "Maybe there's another way. A more press-friendly way of creating a positive buzz—above and beyond the charity ball," he added, nodding at Holly.

"I've done a timeline to chart strategic points for maximum

impact—release of the invitation list, the donors, the theme," Holly said, her mind working quickly to incorporate the revelation of Jake's true identity. "We can hint at an 'important announcement' that will be made at the night's end."

"Why at the end?" Jake asked.

"Because the evening is about the charity auction, not the Blackstones. And it ensures everyone stays to bid. We don't want guests leaving halfway through."

"I don't think that'd be a problem," Ryan said smoothly. "Can it be pulled off in time? And will it work?"

Holly gave a confident nod. "Short of a Blackstone wedding, the press will see through any other attempt to garner favourable publicity."

Ric smiled thinly. "Not planning marriage, are you, Jake?"

As everyone murmured in amusement, Garth said, "That's not a bad idea." All eyes swung to him, but he merely shrugged. "As I was saying, our shareholders aren't just intimidated by Jake's business persona. They're distrustful of a single man in his mid-thirties who hasn't formed any significant romantic attachments. A wedding, even an engagement, is the kind of event that brings people together, as you well know. It's a confirmation of love, honour and commitment, which generates a warm fuzzy glow with the public."

From the sudden drop in temperature, Holly knew everyone was holding their breath. She told herself not to look at him. But Jake was like a car crash; you couldn't *not* look.

When she finally gave in to temptation, she fully expected to see a mask of righteous fury, all tight lines and muscle. Instead, his face was blank.

His game face. She'd seen it when he'd met Max, when she'd quizzed him about his intentions. He kept his thoughts firmly under lock and key. When he finally did speak, the room practically vibrated with restrained anticipation.

"Certainly, marriage is on my ten-year plan."

"Jake, it's not—" Kimberley began. "What?"

"I'll think about it."

After a stunned silence, discussions finally moved on to the charity ball, but Holly couldn't drag her eyes away from Jake. When he wasn't looking, she stared at him, only to be caught not once, but three times, by his mocking green gaze.

Just when she thought she had him pegged… She'd fully expected him to blow that idea out of the water, not to actually consider it. But of course. As she quickly handed out the estimated costings for the ball, she shook her head. He had a ten-year plan. He'd approach finding a wife just like any other business deal. He'd want the best—breeding, looks, class. A privately schooled daughter of some brain surgeon, or a minor royal with centuries of hyphenated ancestors.

As if sensing her mounting turmoil, Jake glanced at her. The small conspiratorial smile teasing his mouth incensed her even more.

Damn the man.

For the next thirty minutes everyone added to Holly's proposal. They all agreed it should be a glitzy, glamorous black-tie event specifically designed to raise awareness of Australia's over-stretched rescue services, and all proceeds would go to AusSAR, the national search and rescue organisation that had led the search for Howard Blackstone's downed jet.

When the meeting finally broke up, Holly quickly gathered her paperwork and was first out the door, desperate to focus on work and not other, more dangerous thoughts.

Jake was James Blackstone. Practically Australian royalty. So out of her league.

She stopped her errant thoughts. Since when had she started to entertain those feelings?

"You and Jake should discuss his press statement," Kim said as she emerged from the room and handed her a piece of paper. "And here's a few more people to add to the guest list."

Holly glanced down at the paper. "Matt Hammond?"

Kim nodded. "Yes. We've got Jake back." She looked pointedly at Jake, who was in discussion with Ric and Ryan at his office door. "It's time to start building some bridges and bring this family together again."

Holly followed Kim's eyes and at that precise moment, Jake looked straight at her. Their gazes immediately locked, held. And in that breathless moment, her skin began to heat, like smouldering embers of a furnace stoking back to life.

His study of her felt different. *She* felt different. More aware of the sensual slide of her shirt over her skin, the way her breath faltered on the intake before coming out in a sigh. The way his eyes, full of exquisite knowledge, skimmed the parts of her his hands had touched. Of course, if she were interested, she'd be preening about now.

No, you're not interested. You are so not interested you'd have to drive across the Great Sandy Desert to even find the signposts telling you where interested was.

Yeah, and his kisses were the worst thing you've ever experienced.

As she stood there arguing with herself, she could feel the air suddenly charge with expectation. The interest and heat in his eyes morphed into full flame, his mouth curving in an intimate smile.

Photos never did him justice. Not that strong jawline, the noble Gallic nose, the high brow. And those intelligent emerald eyes that could make her knees buckle with just one hint of a smile. The smile that transformed his entire face right now into something breathtaking.

"Holly, the press statement?" Kim was saying.

Holly ripped her attention away from Jake, only to light on Kim's amused face. She blinked and picked up a notepad, effectively ducking the woman's shrewd eyes. "You're not handling it?"

"I'll take a look at it, of course. But I trust you with this. Just run everything by me before you release anything."

Holly nodded as guilt flooded in. Yes, Max was blackmailing her, but she'd gotten herself in that position. It didn't matter who was right or wrong; the moment she admitted her guilt, there was a good chance she'd be fired. Worse, the Blackstones had invested in her, had trusted her yet she'd betrayed them. How could she admit that failing to Kim, someone she admired and respected?

She couldn't.

"Time will be tight leading up to the ball," Kim said, "so if you need help, just ask." She paused then said, "You needed to see me about something?"

Holly thought quickly. "Did you want to view the decorations, choose stationery…?"

"If you need a second opinion, I'm happy to give one," Kim said, moving towards the door. "But it's your baby, Holly. I know what you're capable of, so just wow us, OK?"

Holly was rooted to the spot, staring at the glass door as it slowly closed. Kim's supreme confidence should have made her ecstatic. Instead, it wounded her in a dozen tiny cuts.

With a steadying breath she whirled, refusing to let worry control the moment. She'd been entrusted with this so she was going to make damn sure it was a success.

With purposeful strides, she walked into Jake's office. He was refilling the coffee pot, his controlled movements a study in efficiency. She halted as he glanced up, every muscle in her body stilling as a welcoming smile spread his sensual mouth.

Her insides did a weird little flip as she returned his smile, feeling like a teenager, all breathless and jittery around her first crush. Even the childish words "James Blackstone is smiling at me!" ran through her mind until she gave an inward groan and chased them away.

"We need to talk about your press release."

Abruptly his expression cooled. "I have another meeting."

"I understand," Holly said, reluctantly matching his business-like tone. "But we need to make time for this."

"I will. Just not now."

She ignored his curt warning. "Let me at least make a start, like some personal background to go on."

With a scowl, he leaned back in his chair and fixed her with that cool, calm stare. It was almost as if he was trying too hard to remain emotionless, to show her that this didn't matter. But deep down, she knew it did. She knew that men like Jake possessed an almost demonic drive to succeed. The key to success was often found in their past—what they did and didn't have. What they lacked. What they desired most.

"Your mother was a single parent?"

"Yes."

"And?"

In the silence, Holly met his stare unflinchingly. "You have to let me do my job, Jake." She stopped, unashamedly wallowing in that small rush of intimacy she felt from simply speaking his name. "Just tell me whatever you feel comfortable with."

He seemed to debate his answer. With deliberate care he admitted, "Nothing about this makes me comfortable."

"So let me help you," she said gently. "We just need enough info to pre-empt all those intrusive questions. Like, how did you find out you were James Blackstone?"

"What happened with Max Carlton?"

She blanched. "We're talking about you."

"And I'm talking about *you*." He leaned back in his chair. "Why should I trust you when you're hiding something?"

Panic forced her into silence. Just what did he know? Had he seen her with Max at the fashion show? Had he somehow dug something up with his team of investigators and bottomless funds?

He watched her like an animal studied its prey, as if with one wrong move or word she'd be history. Yet memories of Saturday night thundered between them, and just like that, the air turned from strained reservation to electrically charged.

She shoved her chin in the air and forced calm into her voice. "There's nothing going on between me and Max."

He leaned back in his chair, his smile full of male knowledge. "See, there you go again. Lying to me."

She arched her brow. "How do you know?"

"You've got a tell."

"A what?"

"A tell—a facial tic, like a giveaway sign. Cops and lawyers use it. So do conmen. I've studied a few techniques myself."

"Is that why you're so good at winning?"

"That and making sure people can't say no."

Holly crossed her arms. "So what is my 'tell'?"

"Your eyes," he said softly. "They widen a little, and your focus shifts away, dropping to my shoulder or just past my ear."

"Maybe I find your ear fascinating."

His short bark of laughter surprised them both. As she stood there, a reluctant grin on her lips, her heart did that weird little jump again.

Her pen dropped from her nervous fingers and she bent to retrieve it, panic closing her throat. *You want him. He can't know.*

Like a strange rhythmic tattoo, she repeated the mantra in her head until her senses spun from the realisation. With steely determination she straightened, forcing it from her mind.

If you don't think it, he can't read it on your face.

Still, he must have sensed something, because his eyes narrowed curiously.

"Tell me about your childhood," she asked, desperate to deflect his focus. "Where did you grow up?"

With a look that told her he knew what she was doing, he said, "When I was ten, we settled in Tanunda, South Australia. April remarried when I was fifteen."

"Were you happy?"

"Are teenagers ever happy?" When she frowned, he sighed. "Did we have money? No. Life was tough. We moved with whatever seasonal work my mother could get, which always made me the new kid at school."

"I can imagine."

"No, you can't," Jake bit back harshly as the memories tumbled in like a burst dam. "You're from a small town where everyone knows you, where your family has roots, standing in the community. You probably know the bank manager by name and invited the neighbors around for barbeques on the weekend." Unable to contain his agitation any longer, he whirled to face the huge windows. "You weren't called the bastard son of the town's drunken whore."

Her sharp intake of breath sliced at him, bringing fresh pain to the surface. He shut his eyes, forcing the memories back where they belonged.

"I need to be across town in half an hour," he said curtly. "We'll discuss this later. Just…" He waved a dismissive hand, "Just write up what you know and leave the other bits blank. E-mail it to me and I'll fill in the rest."

He then turned to the papers on his desk, riffling through them with single-minded concentration, even as he sensed Holly still standing there, radiating with frustration.

A moment passed, then two and Jake finally looked up. "Is that all?" he queried softly, forcing his expression to reveal nothing of his inner turmoil. Inside, his jaw ached from clenching it so tightly.

Go. Just go.

A look passed over her face—part sorrow, part pain. Before he could say anything, she nodded.

"That's all for now." And she turned and walked out.

At five-thirty Holly sat in Jake's car, being taken to goodness knows where. She twisted the earring around in her lobe, staring out at the passing traffic. Max had called to demand an update, which had forced her to acknowledge their plans for the ball. When he'd sneered, "How noble," it gave her a small perverse satisfaction to say swiftly, "I have work to do. Gotta go," and hang up on him.

Thankfully the ball preparations had then commanded her thoughts elsewhere, away from Max, from her situation. The

Blackstones had placed an almighty trust in her by revealing Jake's identity, given the tenuous grip they had with privacy right now. How could she possibly destroy that trust?

Worry sawed at her composure, leaving her raw and confused. She needed to stall Max until after the ball, after she'd proven her loyalties lay with Blackstone's. Only then could she come clean and get rid of the menacing threat hanging over her head.

She glanced at a silent Jake…James. *James Blackstone.* Sheer amazement had waylaid her at inopportune times during the day. She'd wanted to ask him a dozen questions but hadn't seen him since their press release discussion. Of course he had other things to do, important meetings to attend, small countries to buy out. He wasn't avoiding her.

At least, now he wasn't.

"Tell me again why I couldn't just catch a cab home?" she said as the peak-hour traffic crawled by.

"You saw the reporters outside Blackstone's." She wasn't sure if his sympathetic glance was real or a put-on. "As my rumoured love interest, you *are* news now."

"And me in your car helps how? You *have* read that little article on page ten of today's *Telegraph*, haven't you?"

He waved away her concern with an imperious hand. "We both know you're not having my baby. Unless—" his eyes turned mischievous "—you want to."

She blinked, cramming down the sudden fluttering desire that flared in her belly. "Jake…"

"Relax, Holly." He dismissed her shocked look. "You want my undivided attention for this press release. I'm giving it to you."

Fifteen minutes later, passing through no less than two security gates that required key card and password access, then another keypad at the complex doors, Holly stood in the middle of Jake's elaborate Pyrmont Bay apartment in silent awe. As if sensing her keen interest from the moment she walked in, he'd given her the cook's tour. From the entrance she stepped into an open-plan living area featuring a large fireplace at the far end flanked by two curved couches. To her left was the modern kitchen. His office space was separated by a glass wall. She'd walked down the two steps to the sunken entertainment area, which boasted a massive plasma screen and two single reclining lounge chairs. Beyond ceiling-to-floor windows, a balcony offered a magnificent view of Pyrmont Bay and Darling Harbour.

To her relief he'd nodded to the staircase and said, "Bedroom, spare room and bathroom."

She looked around. The place simply screamed rich single guy. She didn't even notice that Jake had turned on the TV until she saw her face plastered on the six-o'clock news.

"Are you seeing this?" she said softly as he walked past her into the kitchen.

He retrieved a bottle of wine from the fridge. "I caught the midday news."

She stared as he grabbed a corkscrew from the drawer, his nonchalance only cranking up her irritation. "So what are you going to do about it?"

He glanced up at the screen, then back to the cupboard where he removed two glasses. "I'm flattered you think my powers extend to bringing down the world's oil prices."

She scowled. "I'm talking about us. Us. On the news. Having a love affair."

His throwaway smile curled Holly's toes. "We're having a love affair on the news? How Paris Hilton of us."

She took a deep breath and sent a small prayer heavenwards. "Is this funny for you? We're the lead story and that doesn't bother you?"

"No. We're both single, responsible adults. Why should it bother you?"

"Because it's dragging Blackstone's into the limelight again. It's intrusive and inflammatory and they've been through enough."

His expression became astute, as if she'd said something vitally important. "But it's not about them. It's about us— Holly and Jake's clandestine office romance."

She opened her mouth to argue but quickly snapped it shut when realisation dawned. "It's good publicity. For once, the headlines are positive."

"You got it in one."

She perched on the arm of a lounge chair and toed off her heels. "Great. At least they haven't found out where I live." But the look on his face plummeted her scant hope. "You're kidding me."

"Sorry." He offered her a glass and she took it, downing her first gulp of expensive crisp Riesling. Miko's father was going to be pissed. The Tarasais were very private, very conservative...

She abruptly stood. "My parents. They'll freak if—"

"Already taken care of."

"How?"

"I sent a discreet security detail this morning."

Stunned, she sat back down on the couch with a shake of her head. "I can't let you—"

"Sure you can." Even as he casually leaned against the wall, his eyes remained watchful. "You didn't e-mail me your draft release."

With a soft sigh she rubbed her temple. "Because there are too many gaps. I still don't know how you found out you were really James Blackstone."

"My mo— April confessed before she died."

"I see."

Jake shot her a look. "It wasn't a guilty conscience, if that's what you're thinking. Someone in her old town had contacted Howard's P.I.s, and she wanted to tell me before the shit hit the fan."

"So she was protecting you."

His derisive snort came out half-hearted, giving her hope. She tried again. "What was the first thing you bought when you made your first million?"

"Why?"

It almost made her want to weep at the distance in those expressive eyes. "Just go with me on this."

He paused, as if weighing her intentions in that simple question. "A town house for my mother in Lilyfield."

He gave her his back then, turning to the expansive view of the bay. Yet she could see his face mirrored in the smooth glass, the naked emotion twisting his features until his reflected gaze landed on hers. Their eyes held breathlessly for one second, then two…then his expression eased.

He turned back to her and crossed his arms. "She was sick for a long time," he said softly. "Liver cancer, even though she'd stopped drinking years ago."

"But she took good care of you?"

"As best she could. Until I could take care of her. She…"

He paused, and in that small hesitation Holly sensed something, something deep and painful enough to bring a falter to his steady voice, something that still continued to eat away at him.

She watched him rub the bridge of his nose, his eyes dark with remembrance.

"I asked about my father once," he said quietly. "I was about eight. She told me her last boyfriend was abusive. I never asked again."

Holly stilled, the air so motionless she could almost hear the dragging reluctance as he continued.

"I was fifteen when she married John Kellerman. The guy was a nasty piece of work, always drinking, always abusive. I couldn't figure out why she'd stay with someone like that."

"Maybe she wanted to give you stability."

He fixed her with an astute look. "Well, it royally backfired."

It hurt her heart, the sudden and instant vulnerability this man displayed. For all his control, all his power, he was felled by something so simple, yet so complex.

A mother's love.

She glanced at the TV screen, which flickered with images of a devastating south-coast rainstorm. So furious and powerful. Yet when everything was over, devastation and vulnerability.

"You can trust me, Jake."

He straightened, a shutter descending over his features as he abruptly changed the subject. "Are you hungry?"

Through the simple meal of steak and grilled vegetables that he refused help to prepare, he dropped cryptic personal tidbits that were short on emotional detail. It was as if by leaving out embellishment, he could remain detached from it all, a bystander just reeling off the facts. By the end of dessert—a decadent vanilla toffee-chip ice cream—she knew that Quinn's mom had taught him how to boil perfect spaghetti, that he'd invested in nearly every country in the world and that he'd broken his nose twice.

"You'd never know," she said, eyeing his profile as they took a seat on the lounge before the fire.

He ran his finger down the bridge almost absently. "I had it fixed."

"Really?"

"My only concession to vanity," he admitted with a small smile.

Vanity or trying to fix the past? Under Holly's probing gaze, he remained silent until she said softly, "When?"

He met her eyes unflinchingly. "After my stepfather broke it."

She swallowed, emotion clogging her throat as she broke eye contact and glanced around his expansive apartment. It was then she noticed the small array of private objects gathered atop a bookshelf.

"Tell me about those."

She noted the way he studied the items, and instinctively she knew he could catalogue them blindfolded.

Finally he said, "The black stone is from Bells Beach, my first visit. The key is from my first car, a Holden Torana." His smile flickered.

"A list of firsts," Holly murmured. "The boarding pass?"

"First overseas flight." He nodded to one of the two framed photos. "Quinn and I flew to Africa to inspect the diamond mines."

"Must have been a good trip."

At his quizzical glance, she supplied, "You're smiling. You don't do that often."

"Don't I?" he replied absently, his gaze going back to the other photo, older and grainier.

"You and April?"

"Yes. She…" Jake stopped, remembering the brief moment of happiness all too well. "I was eleven. She'd just got a cashier's job at the local 7-Eleven store and we'd gone to the games arcade to celebrate." The seasonal fruit-picking gig had dried up when the rain had, leaving them with barely enough money to eat, let alone feed his mother's alcohol habit. When she'd realised it was either the drink or food for her son, she'd stopped cold turkey.

"Tell me more about her."

At her soft probing, Jake felt a well of trepidation lodge in his gut. "Until I was about ten, we moved a lot. Now I know why." Seeking the comfort of movement, he stood, turning to face the window displaying Sydney's cloudy night sky. "Howard's housekeeper and her boyfriend were named as the kidnappers."

"Yes. Two months after you disappeared, the cops found their bodies. Everyone believed James drowned in that car," Holly said behind him.

Jake nodded curtly, battling with the sudden claustrophobia as he focused on his reflection in the spotless window. "April rescued me."

"Why didn't she turn you in to the authorities?"

Jake closed his eyes as the demons struggled within. "It wasn't that simple. She was on the run from an abusive boyfriend and still suffering the loss of her own baby a year ago. When she pulled me from the car it was like God had given her another chance. At least, that's the way she saw it."

"So she deliberately kept you."

Jake turned at the lack of emotion in Holly's voice. "Yes."

"Didn't she know who you were? That there was a

mother and father out there grieving for a child they thought had drowned?"

Jake's throat constricted. Determinedly he forced the memory up, as if confronting it would somehow negate the fear. Foul-smelling dirty water rushing in through the car window. Him screaming and beating his small fists at the door. Choking, crying.

And then a saviour.

April Vance. His mother for the past thirty-two years of his life. A life that had been ripped away, a potential fishbowl for the world to view and inspect.

"She risked her life to save me."

"That must have taken courage." Holly stopped all pretence of mentally cataloguing his story now. The urge to grab the pad and pen from her bag, gone.

"Yes."

The look on his face was stark. A great man suddenly vulnerable and raw, Holly realised. And past that, she could see reluctance…and embarrassment. He was a man unfamiliar with discussing his deeper feelings, with showing emotion.

Holly's heart ached for him, for the pain of his youth, for the still-to-come scrutiny that he'd have to weather. And on the heels of that came the sudden overwhelming desire to alleviate his pain, to share some of the burden.

Her voice was small when she spoke. "A big-shot buyer promised to bail out my family's company when we got into financial difficulty."

He turned, studying her face carefully, searching for a deeper meaning behind her sudden revelation. Determinedly she continued, "Instead, they bought us out then liquidated. Sacked everyone. Twenty families couldn't afford to feed their children, marriages fell apart, people had to sell their homes and possessions. Some had to leave the town where they'd lived all their lives."

"And you were one of them."

"We stayed. Many didn't. When Dad lost the business, it was the end of him. He just…" she hesitated, pausing to analyse the once-painful memories. "He gave up. The workers blamed him and pretty soon he did, too. I blamed myself."

His eyes turned razor-sharp. "You were seventeen, just a kid."

"I nagged him to sell because I wanted to go to university." She let the remnants of bitter frustration hover in the thick air, waiting for it to dissipate into the silence. After it slowly faded away, she sighed. "After Dad's stroke, Mum gave up too. Their living expenses and medical bills were astronomical—" And her responsibility. The reminder ground the rest of the words to dust in her mouth. "Sorry, I got off track. We were talking about you."

But with a sinking heart she knew the moment was gone. Jake's expression had reverted to his signature control, albeit with a tightness bracketing his mouth.

"It's getting late. I'll get Steve to drive ahead, make sure the press have gone from your place. Do you have enough to draft something up?"

She nodded, knowing there'd be nothing else this evening.

Later, in Jake's car, when she finally had a chance to make sense of her uncharacteristic confession, a terrifying thought began to bloom. With a soft groan, she put her forehead on the cool glass.

Oh no. You can't. Are you actually having feelings for Jake Vance?

Seven

On Wednesday, Jake took a left turn and drove into the exclusive suburb of Vaucluse, then clicked off the ten-o'clock news. As predicted, there had been a flurry of activity following yesterday's press release of the charity ball, with both Blackstone Diamonds and AdVance Corp fielding interview requests for the past hour.

He'd never cared for subterfuge or smokescreens when it came to business, yet he understood the necessity behind it all—protecting Blackstone's bottom line. To their credit, Holly and Kim had done a skilful job of appeasing the public, spending the whole day with the press and on radio, generating interest in the ball and expertly diverting any negative questions.

Behind the steering wheel of his brand-new dark blue Presara, he glanced out the window, noting the barely visible Vaucluse mansions from the road. He counted off the numbers, searching for the right one that would signal his impending meeting with Sonya Hammond.

It was not in his plans, this "getting to know the family" stuff. At least Ryan and Ric had kept it to a minimum, focusing instead on his intentions for Blackstone's. Kimberley had been more of a problem, with her gentle probing and bulldog stubbornness. In that respect, she was like him, a comparison that sent a wave of weird déjà vu scuttling across his skin.

There was no good reason he needed to meet Sonya. Baring his past to scrutiny made crawling over hot coals a more appealing prospect. But despite all his logical reasons why not, there was one big why.

He wanted answers. He needed them. And the not knowing felt like a hole burning away in his gut.

He needed to know about Howard—and not just what the papers reported. He needed to know about his real mother, and whether she'd truly been as miserable as he'd assumed.

So he'd finally agreed to this meeting, much to Kimberley's surprise. "If you hurt Sonya, your life will not be worth living," she'd stated mildly, her glittering emerald eyes hard like the jewels she promoted. He'd merely nodded. Over the past few days, first Ryan, Ric, then Kim had dropped tidbits about Sonya Hammond. They considered her more than just Ursula's sister, more than the mother of Danielle. She was a mother-figure, one who was loved and cherished, who was the backbone of the Blackstone family.

He finally reached the end of the road. Dead ahead lay a set of huge iron gates, accompanied by a discreet security camera on the left. The gates swung inwards without a sound, giving off a final click after he drove through.

It wasn't until he'd exited his car and stood in front of the huge three-story mansion that a wave of apprehension nearly knocked him flat.

Oh, God. The house.

With his eyes he traced the lines of the building, lingering on every window, every angle of the smooth white cement render.

The dreams had mercifully stopped years ago, but now he forced himself to remember the fragments—a large white house with a million rooms, enough for a small boy to hide from a laughing woman with loving eyes. But they weren't dreams, he realised now. They were memories. Memories of this house, of his real mother.

For one incredible second, he was catapulted back in time, back to where his mind jumbled with familiar smells, familiar sights. The sharp, salty tang of the ocean. The warm, grainy sand between his toes.

A hug, the sound of gentle laughter.

He rocked on his heels, fear icing his feet as he struggled, standing there on the expensive parquet driveway, the huge haunting house looming ahead.

Yet amazingly, underneath the panic, a tiny sliver of relief bloomed. Relief that, however far-fetched it sounded, he finally knew he wasn't crazy.

He forced himself to focus, concentrate, to walk forward to the house.

Just like last week, when he'd been hovering on the threshold in the foyer of Blackstone Diamonds, he regrouped. This wouldn't beat him. He'd spent nearly all his life fighting something, from playground bullies to his stepfather, from workmates to competitors.

He was determined to focus on business but this family stuff was freaking him out. His jaw ached from gritting his teeth. This would not beat him.

So why was he so bone-tired from fighting?

He dropped his head, staring at the stonework as a flood of eerie emotions swamped him.

He was the eldest son of Howard Blackstone. Maybe this was where he belonged.

With a determined slant to his shoulders, he walked the small distance between familiarity and the great unknown. But before he could press the doorbell, the door opened and an elegant woman stood before him.

She was immaculately groomed, from the top of her regal head with its pulled-back brown hair, to the blue cashmere sweater and tailored beige pants, to the tips of her brown pointy heels.

A queen, fit to head the Blackstone dynasty, was his first thought. And when he took in her face, he was struck by the warm, welcoming expression, completely at odds with her majestic composure. Then she enveloped him in a generous embrace and his polite greeting fizzled on his tongue.

"James," she whispered as she squeezed him tightly. "You're finally home."

In stunned silence he felt her tremble as she hugged him. For one second, he hesitated. Should he step back? Refuse to come inside? Maintain that crumbling wall of cool politeness he'd reserved for the whole Blackstone clan?

Should, should, should…

The choice he finally made shocked the hell out of him. He embraced her back. And somehow it felt right.

* * *

It was after ten on Friday night, after Jake had negotiated a deal with a New York property development company, that he finally gave his meeting with Sonya a critical going over.

He'd expected the meeting to take an hour, tops. His goal had been to find out what Howard was really like, get a sense of his dead mother, discuss family dynamics. Instead, four hours later he was still there, listening in silent fascination as Sonya recounted personal memories of the Blackstones.

When Sonya had given him a tour of the mansion, he'd finally had an explanation to his haunting dreams. She'd also provided greater insight into Ursula and Howard. Especially Howard.

But for every positive, there were a dozen major character flaws. Howard was a horrible human being, of that he'd had no doubt. The kind of person who collected mistresses then tossed them away like a petulant child with a broken toy.

His fists clenched. There was no way he was like that bastard.

"Did you have a good life, Jake? Were you happy?"

Sonya's soft question, her calm warmth, had undone him. For one horrifying second, he thought he'd break down and blubber like a newborn. Instead he'd forced a smile and replied, "April loved me. That's better than a lot of other kids."

That part was true. He'd wasted his teenage years blaming her for every setback, every disappointment. After he'd clawed his way back on the stock market he'd finally had a chance to right things.

"And what of a family of your own?" she'd asked him. "A wife, children?"

For the second time in as many days, a sudden aching desire slammed into him, astoundingly intense. Everyone close to him had paired off, like partners at a dance and he'd been a last-minute invite. Meanwhile, he'd been trying to fill the void with material things. It was only now he realised he'd been digging in vain.

He needed…something more. Something like he'd glimpsed on Ryan's face. Something he sensed from Kimberley and Perrini.

Unity. A partnership. Trust.

Through the frustration, the desperate want, he kept coming back to the one woman who'd gotten completely under his skin. One who didn't care how many millions he made. One who challenged him, both verbally and mentally, who had tugged violently at his self-control for the first time in for ever.

He walked into the kitchen, the polished floor shockingly cold to his bare feet. After grabbing coffee from the counter he drank deep, the scalding liquid flaming his throat.

He tried to quench a thirst that had nothing to do with his burning desire to make more money, to scale that tentative tightrope of success. Instead, erotic images, like exploding firecrackers, shot through his mind, emptying it of rational thought. He gave himself a mental shake and tried to concentrate on the deal he'd made two hours ago, but all he could think of was a pair of languid eyes and a kissy-mole near the corner of a luscious mouth. How that mouth had tasted beneath his, all warm and wet and pliant. How it would feel on his body, trailing hot kisses over his chest, down his belly, taking him willingly and deeply…

He'd wrenched himself from the fantasy too many times in the past few days. The last time he'd practically bitten off his broker's head. Now his mind whirled as he gave it free rein, his entire body humming with pent-up tension. He could practically feel her beneath his hands, taste her.

Smell her.

With dawning realisation, the denials he'd been wrestling with fell away like dirt washed from a submerged precious stone. He understood one thing with perfect clarity—he wanted Holly.

So what was stopping him?

"Go away. And no comment!" Holly's husky post-sleep growl came crashing over him through the intercom, and suddenly the wave of purpose that had carried him to her apartment drowned in hot desire.

"It's Jake."

She cursed softly. "Do you know what time it is?"

"It's—" he checked his watch "—ten minutes past eleven."

He heard her sharp intake of breath as she battled for calm. In gleeful anticipation, he wondered if she'd win.

In his mind's eye, he envisioned her jumping up from the bed in a flurry, throwing off the blankets, her hair in disarray. Her bare legs hitting cool air and goose-bumping her skin. Her nipples pebbling beneath some kind of red satin nightgown, one thin strap slipping gently off a shapely shoulder.

"What can't wait until Monday?" Holly was saying, her tone indicating she'd already repeated herself while he'd been halfway to fantasy land.

"I need to ask you something."

Holly rubbed her eyes and caught her sigh before it escaped. *Jake Vance needs me.*

She nearly laughed aloud. *Yeah, he really needs me like*

this. She took in her yellow oversize T-shirt and shorts, dotted with huge red hearts.

"Holly, can you just let me in?"

In answer she jabbed the button, grabbed a robe then shuffled to the door, opening it as he emerged from the dark pathway into the porch light.

"You've been working?" She eyed his business attire, her gaze coming to rest on the neckline where he'd loosened his tie.

"And thinking."

"Ahh."

"What?"

She heard the irritation in his voice and smiled. "Too much thinking'll do that." She walked down the hall then turned into the dimly lit kitchen. "About what?"

"I have a proposal for you."

"Which is?" She tightened her robe then glanced up, only to find him looking at her with that single-minded focus. She smiled to cover her nervousness. "What?"

"Marry me."

Eight

"Are you out of your mind?"

His smile petered out. "Not exactly the answer I was looking for."

"You're seriously going to go through with Garth's suggestion? Get married for the sake of Blackstone's?"

"No. I've given this a good deal of thought."

"You obviously haven't!"

"Yes, I have," he countered, eyeing her as she stopped pacing to glare at him. "A wife has been on my list for over a year."

Holly felt her jaw go slack. *Of course it has.* "Why me? Aren't there a dozen other women you could pick from? Supermodels, socialites…"

"I picked you."

Holly's skin prickled in excitement at his possessive declaration. She stubbornly forced it down. "Why?"

"Holly, let me lay this out for you. What I'm proposing is a business deal, pure and simple."

She narrowed her eyes. "What?"

"Hear me out. Romance, love, is unpredictable at best. I believe in attraction, lust. Sex." His eyes darkened as they settled on her lips. "I don't believe there's a power that conquers all. That's just too…"

"Optimistic?"

"Unrealistic," he corrected.

She blinked, weighing his words carefully. She had to know. For some perverse reason, she just had to. "You've never been in love?"

"Once. It didn't amount to much."

The cold cynicism slanting his mouth took her breath away. "With Mia?"

Jake's lip curled in barely hidden contempt. "No. Quinn's foster sister, Lucy."

Lucy? Holly blinked at the unfamiliar name. "So you'd settle for a bought wife."

"I'm not settling. You're everything I need in a wife. I'd be a fool to pass up the opportunity."

Indignation tightened her jaw. "How clever of you. And what do you have that I could possibly need?"

"Money." His eyes turned deadly serious. "I can clear all your debts, buy back your family home and pay respite care for your father." He named a dollar amount that staggered her.

"You…" she breathed, as reality washed over her in an icy wave. This was the kind of man he was. The kind of man who kissed like an angel, had the face of a living god. And who made deals like the devil.

"Your family needs you, Holly. Which means *you* need *me*.

I'm offering you a business deal and you should give it the attention it deserves."

Her heart contracted painfully in her chest. "Marriage is not a business deal. For your information I have other ways of finding that money. I don't need to marry you to get it."

"Really?" He narrowed his eyes, calling her bluff. "How?"

"That's none of your business."

"Does it involve Max Carlton?"

She flushed furiously. "No!"

"Blackstone's?"

"Why would it involve..." She blinked in sudden clarity. "You think *I'm* the press leak?"

Her disgust was so palpably raw, so instantaneous that it shamed him. Her response irrevocably proved her innocence. But despite that, one thought still niggled. "No. But there *is* something going on with you and Max."

She swallowed, her eyes darting past his shoulder. "He was my boss." She looked defiant. "End of story."

Liar. "So why not take my offer?"

Frustrated at her stubborn silence, he crossed his arms. "Fine. Let your parents lose their house. Have them floundering around in debt for the rest of their lives. And keep right on using most of your pay packet to support them."

The hurt in her eyes cut deep but he was too wound up, too hell-bent on getting her capitulation, to let that stop him now.

"You...you..."

"It's the truth. What we have is simple. You agree to be my wife and weather Blackstone's through this mess and I will compensate you so you can set your family up for life."

Holly slowly shook her head, backing away from him. The enormity of this situation, the implications, fluttered around

in her head like swarming butterflies. "I can't think right now.
I..." She swallowed thickly. "I need you to leave. Now."

"Holly."

She crossed her arms, aware how futile her defiance was
in the face of his iron determination. "You can't force me into
this. I need some time."

He searched her eyes, but she steeled herself to reveal
nothing. "Don't take too long," he finally said. "I'll be expecting your answer." And with that he turned on his heel and
walked out.

An hour later, Holly lay on her bed and glared at the
ceiling, phone in her hand.

Despite the time, she'd called home to restore some of the
balance to her careening thoughts, to touch a piece of stability that had been sadly missing since Jake had shown up.
When her mom had answered, a wave of longing washed
over her. Through the brief conversation Holly couldn't help
but think how different everything would be if she was finally
free of the weight of debt.

She loved her family but was so weary from being the sole
responsible one. Her father couldn't help his condition, but
her mother... Her chest tightened, hating the way her thoughts
were headed. The term "enabled dependency" fit her mother
well. She'd simply given up trying to cope and now Holly bore
that burden alone, taking charge of the bill payments, buying
groceries, scheduling her father's gruelling rehab. The exhaustion ate into her very bones, bringing forth a deep ache
to her muscles.

The engaged signal buzzed in her ear, dragging her back
to the present. With a tight throat, she cradled the receiver.

Rolling on her side, she shoved her cheek into the pillow. Pride and honour were two qualities she'd gotten from her dad. From her mum, it was a sense of integrity, a strong and deep respect for family. You stuck by them, no matter what.

She squeezed her eyes shut as uncertainty and fear battled for top honours, yet she had to consider all her options. It didn't change her situation with Max. In fact, it would only make it worse. Heaven knows what he'd do with no leverage against her. But that only made her more determined to extricate herself, to prove her innocence. Damned if she'd play a helpless damsel and let Jake fight her battles. But everything else had changed with one cool proposal. She had to do *something*, anything to save her family.

Jake Vance wants to marry me. The prospect excited as much as it petrified her. She swallowed thickly, shoving an errant curl off her cheek. Was it selfish to actually want this? That despite how concrete her marriage beliefs were she still thrilled at the prospect of having Jake all to herself?

She punched the pillow. He'd seduced her with his mouth and hands, then unknowingly elicited her compassion with his expertly covered wounds. Jake had changed everything, and despite her fervent wishes, she couldn't turn back time.

So if he could enter into this union with business-like clarity, so would she.

As the cab drove her to Jake's apartment complex, she glanced at her watch—one in the morning. Not too late for Jake, who was probably negotiating another million-dollar deal at this very moment. Which was why she was so surprised to hear his husky, sleepy growl after the reluctant security guard had buzzed the intercom.

Her thoughts were confirmed when she walked up the flight of stairs and found him framed in the doorway, waiting for her. She eyed his pajama bottoms, deep creases still indented in the fabric. They were new.

He must sleep in the nude.

She swallowed. Her eyes travelled over the smooth, broad chest, tracing the generous dip and swell of muscle before ending at his shoulders, one of which was leaning on the doorjamb.

"Can I help you?"

His words were mild but his expression was something else entirely. Holly felt the warmth spread from her neck. Another kind of heat—intimate heat—curled in her belly and fanned out. "We need to talk."

He shifted his weight, his arm slipping from the frame. "Come in."

She walked past his half-naked body and only just stopped herself from breathing in deep. Instead she straightened her back and kept going, finally stopping by the fireplace. Heat licked over her body, almost as if trying to ease her apprehension, assure her the decision she was about to make was the right one.

He just stood there, looking rumpled and touchable and so male that she wanted to run her hands over him to make sure he was real.

She crossed her arms. "Is this some strange boardroom game? Revenge against the Blackstones?"

"If I wanted to do that, I'd also want to see those share prices fall. Which I don't."

"Are you sure about this?"

"Isn't that my line?" His eyes creased with humour.

Unbidden, her lips quirked. "I won't quit working."

"I don't expect you to."

"Where will we live?"

"Howard's mansion is now mine."

Rattling around in that huge place…all those rooms… She shook her head. "What's wrong with here?"

He grinned. "Nothing, if you don't mind sharing my bed. I've only got one bedroom."

Holly blinked and flushed, her limbs suddenly becoming languid. "I don't want the press ambushing me at home, taking photos of me collecting the morning paper, digging through my garbage." Her face soured. "Miko's a private person and I won't do that to her."

"Then move in with me." Before she could voice the firm refusal teetering on her lips, Jake cut her off. "You've seen the security. You'll be completely protected."

A shiver tripped down her spine at his supreme confidence. *But who'll protect me from you? Who'll protect…*

"My parents." She stared in sudden acute awareness. "They'll be—"

"They'll be fine. I'll do what it takes to keep them out of it."

Holly's heart contracted painfully. "You're assuming I've said yes."

He crossed his arms. "Haven't you?"

She closed her eyes for a brief second. Where was the romance that she'd dreamed about since she was a little girl? The bended knee, the shaky question from love-filled eyes?

She tamped down her disappointment. *Get a grip, Holly. That's a fantasy. A romantic, unrealistic fantasy.* "I'm saying yes."

"I'll get the contract drawn up." He picked up his phone, punched in a few numbers and issued some orders.

So that's how it was done, Holly thought dazedly. One call, a couple of words and her whole life was irrevocably changed.

The enormity of what she'd just agreed to stunned her so much that she never saw the kiss coming. But in the second that it took for his lips to briefly brush hers, she'd wished he'd never made the effort. It was cold, chaste and very, very business-like.

"To seal our deal," he murmured before withdrawing, taking the heat from his bare skin with him.

You're about to enter into an arranged marriage purely for altruistic reasons. Of course the kiss would be passionless.

So why did she find herself yearning for another, the same one that had stolen her breath with its will-sapping intense heat?

"We'll tell the Blackstones on Monday," Jake said.

Holly paused. "About that. I'd like to keep the details of our arrangement private."

"You want us to fake it?"

She tilted her chin up. "If the truth stays with us, then there'll be no leak. And I need to tell my mum before some reporter splashes it all over the papers."

That sobered him. "You're right. Our success depends on maintaining the charade of romance."

There was something in the way he said that, a definite curl to his lip. "You think romance is a charade?"

"I believe in making logical decisions, not emotional ones. So I'm assuming we have a deal?"

A deal. She dropped her gaze to avoid Jake seeing her dismay. They were so different, so incompatible. Marriage was the culmination of her adolescent romantic aspirations, her fantasies of having it all—a career, a husband and someday, children. Instead she'd made a deal with the devil.

What on earth was she thinking?

It was the look in his eyes, so cool, so business-like. Surely there'd been a time when he'd been a young boy in love, full of hopes and dreams for the future?

She jumped as his firm hand tipped her chin upwards. "Getting cold feet already?" he murmured.

"I have terms." His eyes narrowed and he let her go as she continued, "The full amount you offered needs to be transferred to my account as soon as possible."

"Done." He nodded.

She swallowed. "And I need you to be faithful."

"As in…?"

"No dating other women, no photographs, no cheating. No gossip. It might be a sham marriage, but my family will not suffer for it."

Jake watched the way she tilted her head, proud defiance shimmering in her honest blue eyes.

She'd been the subject of gossip before, first after the Mac-Flight takeover, then the Shipley scandal. He knew she abhorred it.

Which meant, beyond a doubt, that she wasn't the press leak.

When he nodded, the tension in her face ebbed. "How long before we'll see an upturn in the Blackstone shares?" she asked.

"A few weeks, maybe. A good year before it stabilises."

"So that's my stipulation. A year after our wedding date, I'm free to seek a divorce."

Jake raised one eyebrow. "Don't you mean an annulment?"

"An annulment is only if we don't have sex. Oh."

On the tail end of this grin, Holly's face heated.

"Are you planning on having sex with me, Holly? Because

if you are," he continued slowly, obviously enjoying her look of shock, "then I'd be more than willing to accommodate you. Considering my vow to remain faithful for a whole year."

Holly opened her mouth but nothing came out. Until… "You are the most arrogant, conceited—"

He reached out and silenced her with a practised kiss.

The kiss was different again. Not the cool, perfunctory one of seconds ago. Not the punishing one of Saturday night, full of anger and barely leashed frustration.

No, this one was a lesson in seduction, a leisurely exploration of her mouth, designed to specifically arouse.

A guarantee of things to come.

He nibbled her bottom lip as his strong hands cupped her face. Gently, he took his time, increasing the pressure and intensity until desire began to thump in her blood and her eyes fluttered closed.

This was more like it.

She settled up against him willingly, wanting to feel him, to melt into the hot promises his kisses offered.

It amazed her that her body responded to his so surely, so completely. But it was thrillingly, terrifyingly wonderful.

"Stay."

She groaned at his soft command. She attempted to swallow, but her throat was suddenly thick. Instead she looked away, trying to hide the desperate desire no doubt written on her face. For all her hesitation, all her fears, the look in his eyes was real. Her body tingled.

"I can't."

"Can't or won't?"

She closed her eyes as his soft breath ruffled a curl across her cheek and his insistent arousal pressed firmly against her belly. "I can't. I'm going home tomorrow. It's Mother's Day on Sunday."

She felt the exact moment he withdrew. A withdrawal that had nothing to do with his physical position and everything to do with his mindset.

He nodded curtly, running a hand over the back of his neck. Fascinated, Holly watched the corded muscle in his arms flex and release. "You can take my jet."

"Your…?"

He smiled without humour. "Get used to it, Holly. Steve will pick you up in the morning and fly you home. No arguments."

Nine

Late Sunday night, Jake was there to meet her after the plane touched down at the private airstrip. Holly couldn't stop the thrill of pleasure bubbling up at the sight of him. There was no doubt he was a powerful presence in the boardroom, but now, dressed in jeans, emerald sweater and a black leather jacket, that power kicked over into crazy-dangerous territory. It took all her control not to reach up and run her palm over his five-o'clock shadow, to feel the rasp of skin on skin.

It was an ominous portent that excited yet terrified her.

"I told my parents," she said as the car sped them through the clear, cool night. Her lips tilted briefly, as she remembered her mother's excited face, one that had paled then flushed in shock when she realised just who her son-in-law was going to be. Holly even thought she'd seen a flicker of emotion in her father's well-worn face, a face devoid of expression for so many years. "She wants to meet you."

"Of course." Her surprise at his quick acceptance must have shown on her face. "What?" He studied her carefully. "You don't want me to?"

"No. Yes." She untied her tongue. "That is, if you want to."

He nodded. "I want to."

A moment passed between them then, a deeply intimate moment that Holly seized like a desperate woman, tucking it away.

Then he looked away and the moment was gone.

When she returned to the view, she frowned. "This isn't the way to my place."

"The press are still sniffing around. We're going home instead."

Home. She barely had time to be annoyed at his autocratic assumption before they were there. When she reached the doorway to his apartment, her legs were leaden with trepidation. At his enquiring look, she shook away the anxiety and stepped over the threshold, shrugging off her jacket and hanging it on the coat rack.

She was going to be living here and Holly couldn't quite believe it. He was James Blackstone, heir to untold wealth and fortune, holder of extraordinary power. But he was also a man—an amazing, strong, complex man who would soon become her husband.

"First room on the left," Jake called as she mounted the stairs. With a sigh she dumped her bag near the brand-new double bed, the sigh ending in a little gasp as she walked into the ensuite.

It wasn't the gorgeous clawed marble bathtub that surprised her, nor the clean blue-on-white tiling or the skylight that twinkled in the dim light. It was the toiletries lining the elegant vanity—brand-new versions of her moisturiser, her cleanser, her hair mousse. She blinked and smiled, then turned on the shower.

She moved into his spare room silently, but Jake felt her presence more keenly than ever before. When he came up to ask if she wanted coffee, he saw that she hadn't touched anything, not even rearranged the chairs or removed one book from the shelf, yet it was as if her essence had seeped into every piece of furniture in his apartment. The faint, fresh smell was everywhere now, not just at work or in his car. She'd not only invaded his thoughts, but now she was in his space and it suddenly felt like nothing was his any longer.

It felt comfortable.

With coffee cup in hand she settled on the far corner of his couch. She was barefoot, dressed in jeans and a dark blue sweater in some soft material that clung to her curves, and the intimacy of having her in his place, on his couch, speared him low.

Yet the intimacy was tempered with a small but definite amount of tension. He watched her carefully over the rim of his cup, noting the way she fidgeted with her hair. Hair that wasn't tied up in a ponytail, he noticed. It fell around her shoulders, shiny, curling at the ends, demanding to be touched.

"When we visited Daniel's grave on Sunday…there was a new headstone. You didn't have to do that. Thank you, Jake."

He quickly shook himself from the fantasy. "It just seemed like the right thing to do."

"With money so tight, we couldn't afford a decent one."

"I know."

He nodded then cursed inwardly at his lame response. Instead of taking guilty pleasure from the heartfelt gratitude shining her eyes, he should be saying something, doing something…

And then, in a wave of singular clarity, he knew exactly what needed to be said.

"I used to have nightmares."

Holly stilled, unable to move for fear it would jinx the moment. "About?"

"Driving when it was teeming with rain. I can hear the sound it makes on the roof right before we plunge headfirst into a river. I hurt my neck from the whiplash."

Holly held her breath and her head began to spin.

"The water…is dark and foul." His voice came out husky and raw, almost like a great pain seeped from his heart. "It leaks into the car from the broken front window. I bang on the windows but can't get out. I try and try but my hands start to hurt and—" He voice faltered and suddenly there was silence.

It shattered the intimacy so suddenly that Holly reeled from the shock.

When he finally spoke, her chest ached at the cool distance in his clipped tone. "I'm sorry. It's late. You should go to bed."

She watched him stand abruptly while her heart pounded in her throat. There was no way she could sleep now, not with what he'd just said running crazy circles in her brain. He'd given her an amazing intimacy, more intimate than that night in his office, when his lips had been on her mouth, his fingers buried deep inside her.

This powerful, proud, untouchable man had shared something. Which meant she'd discovered a little part of his soul, too.

That thought thrilled her, almost too much.

"No. Stay with me."

Jake was frozen to the spot for one long second, then slowly he turned.

"Stay with me," she repeated, stepped forward to press her body against his, ending his denial on a groan. Her chin tilted up, the look in her eyes pure wanting.

She wanted him.

"Holly—" With a soft curse, Jake relinquished the thin grip on his control.

Like a man deprived of water for weeks, he covered her mouth with his, drinking deeply of her warmth, her compassion.

When her tongue slipped gently between his lips, a low growl of possession erupted from deep within. He crushed her up against him as if he could absorb her directly into his skin.

He wanted to be buried in this woman's passion. Now.

In one swift movement he lifted her in his arms and strode purposefully out of the room, her arms wrapped around his neck.

Mere seconds—or was it a lifetime?—later, he shouldered open the bedroom door and laid her on the bed, his attention never leaving her face as he stripped. Reclining on bent elbows, she watched him with a knowing smile, all tease and promise. All woman. Her eyes grazed over his skin, an erotically charged caress.

Arousal came on hot and strong.

"Strip."

His harsh command sent a thrill of anticipation through every nerve ending in Holly's body. She did, and in record time she was standing there in only a pair of white bikini panties and a matching push-up bra.

When she reached behind for the clasp, he grabbed her arms and shoved her back on the bed.

"Leave it."

And then he was covering her, his long, lean body of granite muscle and hot flesh easing up then settling into her dips and curves.

They fit perfectly.

His hand covered her breast, her nipple eagerly tightening under his smooth caress. With a guttural growl, he gently eased the satin down until both her breasts spilled over the top, a delicious display for his hungry eyes.

Cupping her soft flesh, he took his time, tasting first one, then the other. His mouth and teeth grazed the hard little buds, sucking them into peaks, before pulling back and blowing gently on the swollen nipples.

Ribbons of exquisite sensation wrapped her entire body, swaddling her tingling flesh. His hands were built for loving, for pleasure. And she revelled in it until the throbbing between her legs became unbearable, and she squirmed, needing to find relief.

All she found was his hard arousal nudging at her belly.

She groaned. "Jake, please."

He looked up at her with a wicked gleam in his eye, his mouth still surrounding one breast, teeth grazing, tongue flicking. She couldn't bear it any longer!

Then, finally, he said, "Since you asked so nicely…"

With hot need throbbing away in his veins, Jake reached down and dragged aside the damp fabric of her panties.

He heard Holly gasp, an erotic sound of excited eagerness.

Not yet, my love. Not yet.

When he placed his mouth to her hot damp curls, she

nearly bucked right off the bed. With a firm hand he grasped her hips, holding her in place. And then slowly, sensuously, he proceeded to love her with his tongue.

For a million seconds Holly couldn't breathe. She was one raw nerve, tingling and hot from Jake's mouth, from his breath fanning the fire between her legs, from his soft tongue, licking, caressing the tiny bud that made her quiver and shudder every time he rolled over the sensitive flesh.

She wanted to faint from pleasure. Instead she screamed as the desperate flood of release crashed into her body, drowning her in a wave of ultimate bliss.

Before she could recover, Jake had eased up beside her and was kissing her, her salty taste shockingly intimate on his lips.

She drove her fingers in his hair, revelling in the silky smoothness, joyous that he was all hers to touch, to taste. She wanted to do all that and more, to show him that if he'd only let her, they could have a real future together.

"Jake," she whispered, her breath ragged when he finally, gently, eased his finger into her tightness, still wet from her climax.

Jake clenched his jaw, trying desperately to cling to control, even as he felt it slipping away. With gritted teeth he reached for the nightstand, cursing as he fumbled with the condom packet before she impatiently shoved his hands away and completed the task in record time.

Finally he poised above her, devouring the sight of her peaked nipples, the hot passion in her eyes. With a shuddering breath and a fervent prayer, he plunged deeply.

Colors swirled behind his eyes, creating a maelstrom of sensation. He felt the hot slickness of her muscles surrounding him, the eagerness in her lips as their tongues mingled in erotic mimicry. She smelled divine, an innocent scent mixed with the musky decadence of sex.

She whimpered, almost as if the feeling was unbearable. Yet still her hips rose to his, meeting him stroke for stroke, urging him on. Her gasps as he drew back nearly did him in, but he forced his body to maintain a steady rhythm inside her.

He was on fire, the flames licking at every inch of his skin, pulsing and throbbing.

But he wanted more. Needed more.

He grasped her legs, wrapped them around his waist and plunged deeper.

Holly's eyes opened wide. She realised she was gripping his shoulders, clinging to him the way a drowning victim clings to a life raft. His face was a study in erotic intensity. Those green eyes glowed, full of blazing desire and heat. The muscles in his taut jaw eased and tensed with every soft moan of pleasure he dragged from her.

When he took one nipple in his mouth, grazing her with his teeth, she lost it.

Release, long and loud, erupted from her lips. Through her climax she felt him shudder, as he too, finally took his pleasure.

Much later Holly lay on her back, Jake's rhythmic breathing on her nape, his hand curled possessively around her breast. With a slow, shuddering breath, she let the tumbling emotions wash over her, a blissful wave that paradoxically thrilled and frightened her all at once.

There was no way she could deny it. She loved him.

Jake muttered in his sleep, his hand moving gently over her skin. Her eyes widened as her body leapt to life underneath his touch.

Even now she wanted him. Again.

Slowly, almost teasingly, his palm began to move over her nipple.

She drew in a trembling breath and squeezed her eyes shut, only to hear his rumbling chuckle.

Her eyes snapped open to meet his, and she encountered the smoky desire in those emerald depths.

Later she'd sort through what this all meant. Right now she turned to cover his grinning mouth with her own. Right now this powerful, proud, amazing man wanted her.

"Engaged."

Holly nodded as Kim stood from behind her desk and repeated the word again like an incantation. "That was…" Kim hesitated then looked Holly straight in the eyes and said carefully, "Sudden."

"Sometimes you just have to seize the day." Jake took Holly's hand, nearly startling her, and smiled.

Holly swallowed, caught up in the glow of that one simple action, the way Jake's face transformed into something that stole the uncertainty from her lips. How good an actor was he?

She returned his smile, which he took in his stride, squeezing her hand in acknowledgement.

"Well, Jake is nothing but unpredictable," Kim finally said, walking over to place a congratulatory kiss on Holly's cheek. When she pulled back she scanned Holly's face, her eyes radiating concern.

Holly offered a smile and met her look head-on. "Given the time frame, we should announce it a week out from the ball."

At Kim's silence, Holly added hastily, "You've seen the

media with this. We want the ball to get as much publicity as possible before diverting attention elsewhere."

Kim nodded and sat on the corner of her desk. "OK. I've e-mailed you the final guest list, so after the invites go out, you can make that public. If you need anything, let me know."

"Thanks." For one second, she thought Kim would add something more, but instead, she let them go without further interrogation.

"Do you think she bought it?" Jake asked her as they walked down the corridor to their office.

"Probably not."

"I wanted to tell her the truth."

"No."

"Why not?"

Holly walked through the glass doors, her back straight. "Because it's embarrassing, OK? Normal, well-adjusted people date, fall in love and get married. They don't coldly sign a contract for mutual gain."

He smiled at her indignation. "You're one of the most normal, well-adjusted people I've met, Holly."

"Am I?"

She didn't need to be a mind reader to work out just what was going through his head as they stood there. She blinked slowly, desperate to hide her expression, but her body betrayed her. She felt the heat bloom across her cheeks, spreading languorous warmth into her limbs.

Just when she thought he was about to say something, his phone rang. He flipped it open, said, "I'm on my way," and dropped a perfunctory kiss on Holly's cheek before he strode out the door.

Her fingers traced the rapidly cooling warmth where his

lips had just met her skin. The smallest remnants of a tingle forced her heart into a loping thud-thud.

She'd been dismissed. And just as quickly, her heart began to pound in irritation.

She tried not to let it get to her, to focus on the ball prep-arations, but like a nasty, annoying itch she kept returning to the irritation. Was this an indication of things to come—an abnormal marriage, made from an abnormal deal?

She'd be a professional wife, all show and smiles, Jake's escort to all the proper functions. There would be no intimacy outside the public eye, no sudden romantic gestures, no happy-ever-after dreams that she'd envisioned all her teenage life. No promises of everlasting love.

Why should that upset her?

She squeezed her eyes shut and breathed deeply. *You need to get real, Holly. That's not going to happen.* There'd be no physical contact, unless she told him she wanted it, like last night.

She jolted, her eyes snapping open.

Oh, she wanted it. Badly. But could she walk away after a year was over?

Enough. You need to focus on the here and now. With a de-termined straightening of her shoulders, she reached for the phone and dialled.

"So what's the big secret?" Jessica asked after they'd both collected their lunches and taken a seat near the sun-drenched windows overlooking busy George Street.

"Why do you think I have a secret?" Holly glanced around the Blackstone's cafeteria before biting into her chicken salad sandwich with gusto. Jessica's eyes followed hers.

"That's the only reason we're here at two o'clock, long after the lunch rush. Why you chose this table, away from everyone else…" She dropped her voice low. "You're not pregnant, are you?"

Holly nearly spat out her food. In a flurry of coughing, she grabbed the bottle of water as Jessica gently patted her back.

"No," she finally choked out.

"Well, it has to be something big to warrant this sudden meeting. Not that I don't enjoy our infrequent lunches," Jessica said quickly. "But I know you're flat out with this ball, and handling Jake Vance can't be a walk in the park." She picked up her spoon and dipped it into her pumpkin soup. "How's that going, by the way?"

Holly hesitated, telltale heat prickling her skin. "Busy."

Jessica smiled. "It's OK, Holly. Ryan told me."

He did? "How does he know?"

Now it was Jessica's turn to be confused. "About Jake being James?"

"Oh."

"What did you think I meant?"

Holly took a bite of her sandwich to stall. Jake had been at AdVance Corp all day and whether she wanted to admit or not, she'd missed him. Her thighs tingled at the memories of last night. How he'd made her feel. It had been simply… amazing. He certainly had the Midas touch when it came to pleasing a woman. And he was all hers for a whole year. That thought sent a decadent thrill through her.

A year. Twelve months. Fifty-two weeks. Three hundred and sixty-five days.

She focused on the tabletop and took a thick swallow. No. It wouldn't be all Jake, all the time. He led a busy life that centred around making money, not keeping a wife happy. She was purely there to bolster Blackstone's standing and she had gone into it willingly, with eyes wide open.

"So that's it."

"What?" She refocused on Jessica, who was now grinning like an idiot.

"You've got a thing for Jake Vance."

Denial teetered on the tip of her tongue, the second before she realised that she needed Jess—in fact, everyone—to believe she and Jake had fallen madly in love in less than two weeks.

"Well…"

Jessica leaned in conspiratorially. "I saw that look. Your insides went all gooey just thinking about that six-foot-four hunk of corporate muscle."

"Power does not turn me on," Holly said primly, picking out a piece of tomato from her sandwich.

"Well, must be those eyes, then. That face. Hmm…have you kissed him yet?"

"Jess…" Holly squirmed in her seat.

"You have! I knew it. Tell me."

Holly took a breath and said slowly, "It's a bit more than that."

"Ooh, a scandal!"

"He asked me to marry him."

Jessica's spoon clattered to the floor. "No."

"Yes!" And despite herself, she felt the wide grin from ear to ear.

Jessica grabbed her hands, her joy evident. "This is wonderful! I'm so happy for you!"

At last, a reaction that was worthy of such a life-changing event. A rush of relief flooded her, easing the tension from her spine. "Thank you."

"I thought I saw something between you two at the store," Jess teased. "Have you told your parents?"

"Yesterday. I don't think Mum can comprehend it. She asked when Jake was coming to visit."

"That'll be a culture shock," Jessica murmured.

An understatement, Holly thought as Jessica started on which bridal magazines to stock up on, who would be available to cater, decorate, design. And for once, Holly shoved away the gloomy realities and instead let Jessica's excitement buoy her.

Ten

It was 6:22 p.m. when Holly walked out of Blackstone's delivery entrance to hail a cab. She knew the exact time because she'd been fiddling with the full-color screen of her brand-new mobile phone prototype that Emma in Design had thrust upon her earlier.

"Five megapixel camera, voice recording, Internet access… encrusted with Blackstone diamonds, of course!" the girl had enthused.

"How much is it worth?" Holly had breathed, fingering the stone-studded buttons.

"This one's only a prototype. The stones are CZs instead of real diamonds. It's for the woman who has everything."

Now Holly grimaced as she scrolled through the function buttons. Was she officially a woman who had everything?

Well, you do have Jake Vance. Most women would kill for that.

She nearly dropped the phone when someone suddenly grabbed her arm.

"Max! What are you—" She snapped her mouth shut at the dark anger contorting his face.

"I've been hearing things, Holly. Interesting things. About you and Jake Vance."

He furtively glanced about, alerting her to the fact that the dock was deserted. She was alone with Max in a darkened alleyway, away from prying eyes. She swallowed her apprehension and hoisted her bag on her shoulder.

"What things?"

A sharp wind blew past and he shoved his hands in his pockets. "How you and he are getting along a little too well."

"So?" She blinked. "The papers are full of that stuff. Doesn't mean they're right."

"Oh, I know the difference between fact and fiction." He gave her a devious grin, full of malicious intent. "I have proof."

Holly's mouth went dry. "Proof?"

"Does Wednesday night, executive elevator, ring any bells?"

Holly's heart swelled up, pounding in the back of her throat. Through the shock she saw Max smile. "Funny, I'd never peg Vance for a ten-minute guy. But then, I have intimate—" his eyes swept her body appraisingly "—knowledge of you. He probably couldn't control himself."

Shock yielded quickly to anger. "What do you want?"

"You focusing on our deal," he snapped. "Vance has been meeting secretly with the board and the Blackstones. The bastard's trying to get proof so he can fire me. And if he does, I'll bring you down, Holly. Don't doubt that. All it takes is one phone call and you'll have a dozen reporters on your doorstep."

"I already have," Holly snapped, her heart skipping a beat. "What else can you say that hasn't already hit the papers?"

Max rocked back on his heels, a triumphant gleam in his eyes. "Oh, I reckon the public would be interested to hear all about our little liaison. Especially now that you and Vance are bedmates."

The sharp crack of her palm meeting his cheek echoed in the cold air. The imprint of her hand slowly reddened before Holly's disgusted eyes, her shock only confirming what Max already knew. He barked out a triumphant laugh, a horrible "gotcha!" sound at her look of horror.

"It's funny—you getting cozy with the same guy who's blocking your transfer."

Max's verbal bomb exploded deep inside her. As she numbly shook her head, he shrugged. "When I asked Kim for an update, she said Jake put a hold on your transfer indefinitely."

"I don't believe you!"

"Go ask him. Oh, and that slap will cost you, babe. You and your boyfriend. Ten thousand to start. Or I'll release the tape to the papers."

The press. Oh, my...

The pieces suddenly fell into place with a resounding click. "You!" she said. "*You're* the press leak."

He gave her a slow, controlled clap. "Well done, Holly. My own secretary the first to figure it out. Pity you can't do anything about it."

"Why, Max? You have a good job, an excellent job. What on earth made you betray the Blackstones' trust?"

He gave her a scathing look. "Howard Blackstone thought he was so bloody untouchable with his boardroom politics and holier-than-thou kids. The man had a string of women yet he had the nerve to include a morality clause then lecture me on personal ethics, to reprimand me for sleeping with his staff. It was none of his bloody business."

"So you leaked stories to the press to get back at him. The plane crash. Kimberley's wedding…"

"Yep. And soon the sordid details of Holly and Jake's little affair." His eyes gleamed. "It'll be the lead on every news channel in the country, possibly even the world."

"Unless Jake pays up."

"Unless he pays up. And you, babe," he added, his expression turning triumphant, twisting his features into a snarl, "are my leverage."

Jake knew the moment Holly turned up on his doorstep that something was wrong.

"Why are you blocking my transfer?" she gritted out as she strode inside.

He closed the door with a gentle click then pointed the remote at the television. The split screens flickered off.

"Who told you?"

"Max."

"Ah."

"So? Is it true?"

"Yes."

She shot him a look of pure venom laced with haughty pride.

"Why? Why would you do that?"

"Why are you suddenly concerned about what that man says?"

"Because I've just spent ten minutes listening to his demands. And don't change the subject. Why—"

"What demands?"

"He has a security tape of us in the elevator."

"I see."

The angular lines of his face tightened and she breathed in quick, sharp. "He's also the press leak."

She waited for rage to explode, but all she got was a raised eyebrow. Jake said, "That I suspected."

She blinked. "You did?"

He nodded. "I've had him under surveillance. And I've been meeting with the board outside Blackstone's. It's amazing what people will let slip when they're relaxed and on their own turf." He reached for the phone and dialled.

"What are you going to do?"

"Get him arrested."

After a few minutes, he hung up and swung to face her with a considering look. "Is that all?" he asked softly.

She blanched. "Why?"

"Because a tape of us does not make for a huge scandal, considering we're now engaged. What else does he have on you?"

She tried to swallow past the lump in her throat. "Does it matter?"

"It matters."

She closed her eyes briefly then opened them again, meeting his steely gaze without flinching. "When I was working for Max I slept with him, OK? I breached my morality contract. A dumb, stupid thing to do. Then I put in for that temporary PR job and thought he'd let me go but..." She trailed off in the face of his cool silence. "You knew, didn't you?"

"Max enlightened me about your relationship when I fired him yesterday."

"He—" Holly swallowed a thick wad of disgust in her throat. "Did he also tell you he was blackmailing me to spy on you?"

"No." It wasn't the matter-of-fact way he'd said that one small word; it was the flash of suspicion crossing his face. "Did you tell him anything?"

Her heart plunged. "If I said no would you believe me?"

Doubt was quickly replaced by a cold, remote expression, so eerily familiar that it cut her more surely than Max's threats ever could. "So why bother asking? You've already made up your mind."

His uncertainty in her innocence wounded her to the core. Hadn't she gone against every deeply held belief she had and said yes to a marriage, even when she knew it'd only end in failure a year from now? Didn't he realise how much it had taken for her to say yes?

You love him.

At that tiny spark of realisation, her whole body leapt with joy. But just as quickly, pain sent it crashing to the ground. No. She couldn't. She wouldn't. How could she fall in love with a man who would never return it? A man who thought marriage was just another requirement to tick off on his to-do list, who had brokered it to save a company?

A company you love, her conscience niggled. A company where you felt you belonged, working with people whom you've come to like and respect. But all that didn't mean squat, not when Jake was standing right there, waiting for her to say something, as if daring her to prove her wild claims.

Slowly she withdrew the mobile phone from her coat and gently placed it on the kitchen bench. "I'm not lying, Jake. Here's your proof."

Her dignified exit was foiled when he grabbed her arm before she could reach the door.

With a sharp hiss she twisted, only to still at the serious look in his eyes. "Stay. Let me hear this first."

"I'll be out on the balcony." Craving the cold, sharp bite of air, Holly opened the sweeping glass doors and walked outside. Behind her, in the cavernous silence, she could hear her tinny voice as Jake played back the recording of her and Max in the alleyway.

Ten minutes later Jake had managed to put a lid on his simmering anger as he crossed the threshold to the balcony. The sight of Holly framed against the darkening storm clouds stopped him short. She was propped against the railing, her forehead resting on her arms as they hung limply over the edge. It was the stance of someone close to defeat, to complete and utter exhaustion.

In the blink of an eye, his anger dissipated, whatever details he'd been about to demand escaping his lips in a small sigh.

"Why didn't you come to me with this?"

She raised her head abruptly but didn't turn around. "It was personal. What we have is purely business."

A band of something he couldn't define tightened around his chest.

She turned then, crossing her arms. "So you believe me."

Lord, she unmanned him with her searching eyes. He swallowed. "Yes."

The intensity of her relief surprised him. Yet it also revealed that she needed him to believe she was innocent, that his trust meant something to her.

He'd never thought that one person's opinion could count for so much, could affect him so profoundly. And in that moment, pleasure swamped him.

"Max said you were refusing to approve my transfer."

Her soft statement, devoid of accusation, sent a shot of guilt along his spine. "You've heard the expression, Keep your friends close, your enemies closer?"

"Jake. I'm not—"

"I sensed something going on between you and Max, something you were hiding." He dragged a hand through his hair then rubbed the back of his neck, pausing to warily eye her. She remained still, her expression shadowed by the cloudy night sky. After a brief hesitation, he said brusquely, "I promised the Blackstones I'd find their leak."

Guilt tore at Holly's conscience. Jake was so used to running his own show that explaining himself was obviously foreign to him. It showed in every line of his scowl to the harsh gruffness of his voice.

"I'm sorry," she said, "but I needed to save my job. For my family." She stared across the water, at the dancing lights of Sydney. "I know it's no excuse but—"

Jake covered her cold hands in his. To her amazement the simple touch exuded comfort.

"You're a strong woman, Holly," he said at length.

"Not out of choice."

His eyes met hers in gentle acknowledgement and Holly held her breath, one second, two, before voicing the question teetering on her tongue.

"Tell me about your mother."

He abruptly broke eye contact. For one unbearable moment Holly thought he was going to shut her down. *Don't, don't, don't. Tell me because you want to, Jake. Not because you have to.*

When he finally spoke, his voice was so low the air practically vibrated. "April drifted with the seasonal work—fruit picking, mostly. Then cash-in-hand stuff like cleaning and bar work. I remembered being on the road a lot, different houses and rooms, YMCAs, lots of take-away places.

"One time I asked why we always had to leave." He sucked in a slow breath as though the admission pained him. "I can still hear her voice, see the sadness in her eyes, almost as if she were ashamed. 'Because I'm afraid of what will happen if we get caught,' she said. I assumed it was about her abusive boyfriend. We finally stopped running when I was ten."

"South Australia."

"Yeah. In a town that never fully accepted her." Jake remained silent for the longest time, torn between the wisdom of keeping silent and the desperate need to finally have done with it. With clenched fists he took the first terrifying step and forged on.

"By the time she married, I was uncontrollable, on the path to a criminal record. Maybe she needed to be loved. Maybe she thought I needed a father figure—who knows. So she married an abusive drunk who spent all their money on cigarettes and liquor."

"So you left home."

He nodded. "I was a frustrated, angry kid, desperate for a place to belong. I felt...alone, like a stranger in a foreign country. Like I was destined for something else. No one understood that, least of all April. We argued about me leaving. I didn't want to be her only reason for staying sober. And I couldn't save her unless she wanted to be saved. So I left.

"I ended up in Sydney with three dollars to my name and a chip on my shoulder the size of a skyscraper. After the small-town gossip, the city was a relief. A huge, concrete metropolis of anonymity. Without any money, I was taken in by Quinn's parents, into their halfway house in Newtown."

"Where you met Lucy."

He nodded. "We were together for seven years, until the whole Jaxon Financial thing. It took all my money to clear my name, and suddenly she didn't want to be with someone who was broke. Recovering from that betrayal was one of the hardest things I've ever done."

Her hand on his arm was soft, the touch reassuring. It unmanned him.

"Then came Mia."

"Yes." His mouth twisted. "My assistant who lied and cheated."

"Did your mum know where you were after you left?"

He swallowed and closed his eyes. "Not for ten months."

"Oh, Jake."

Her abject sadness pierced his heart. "Believe me, it's not something I was proud of."

"But you eventually made it up to her. That counts for something."

He pressed his fist to the cold metal, trying to grind out the fresh pain welling in the old wound.

As Holly watched him standing there, a solitary figure surrounded by wealth and success, struggling with his inner demons, her compassion took an abrupt detour, morphing into something warmer, deeper. Scarier. It bloomed slowly, cautiously in the corner of her heart she'd reminded herself never to relinquish until she was positive she couldn't be hurt again. But her emotions were far from listening to reason. Her heartbeat quickened, her breath became shallow, her skin heated.

Here was a man who desperately needed to be loved. His

eyes might radiate coldness, a calculating coldness that fooled most, but not her. In every stern line on his granite face, every steely tension in his muscles, she knew.

It would take a special woman to break through that tightly leashed control. She knew what she was up against—the ghosts of women past had not been kind to Jake Vance. They'd made him who he was—distrustful of emotion, determined not to take risks.

She nearly laughed aloud. His whole life was about taking risks...except when it involved love.

Oh yes, he was a long shot. But what did she have to lose? Her heart? No, he already had that. But if she didn't at least try, then she'd never know.

"I have something for you," he said softly, shattering the silence.

She waited as he dug around in his jacket pocket. When he produced a velvet box Holly felt the breath catch in her throat.

She took it, eased open the lid. And gasped.

She recognised the ring from the Blackstone's store—a simple square-cut sapphire on a plain gold band, surrounded by tiny diamonds.

When she finally met his eyes, the uncharacteristic uncertainty on his face stunned her.

"I know it's not exactly how you thought this moment would be, Holly, but—"

"It's perfect. How did you know?"

He smiled an odd, almost gentle smile. "You stared at this ring for far too long."

She smiled back, and despite the reality of what she'd agreed to, emotion clogged her throat.

He must have sensed that because, with a barely hidden

flash of alarm, he removed the ring from the box, grasped her hand and slipped it on.

A perfect fit.

His hand lingered on hers, yet when she looked up at him, he'd erected his wall so quickly that Holly could almost see it going up brick by brick. And it was so expertly made that it made her want to weep. How could she ever break that thing down, when it had taken him years to construct and perfect it?

By showing him with the only thing that felt true, that temporarily dismantled all his defences, all his barriers.

She took a deep, shuddering breath before she leaned in and kissed him.

Eleven

The remaining days leading up to the charity ball passed in one big blur. Holly felt as if she were walking on air, as if sheer joy radiated from her like a tiny sun. First Jessica, then Kim, had commented on her "bridal glow," a comment that brought an embarrassing flush to her cheeks.

As expected, their engagement announcement the week before had prompted an almost obscene amount of publicity. Blackstone's had been inundated with requests for interviews, photo shoots, exclusives. And every time, Jake had told her to refuse them. Their silence only exacerbated the mysterious secrecy surrounding their initial announcement, which, from a publicity point of view, couldn't have been more perfect in its timing. Instead of takeovers and Jake's chequered past, the papers were now speculating on wedding dresses, honeymoons and whether the charity ball was really a cover for their secret wedding reception.

As Jake had promised, Max was charged with multiple contract violations and issued with a gag order. "Along with some subtly aimed threats," Kim had confided to Holly. To Holly's amazement, she and Kim had quickly formed a strong bond, sharing more than just business-related topics as they worked towards the impending date of the charity ball. Jessica had also made a habit of lunching with her every Friday, which touched Holly more deeply than she wanted to admit.

It was bittersweet, this sudden and immediate acceptance into the Blackstone clan, yet she refused to dwell on the wider implications. For once in her life she wasn't planning, scheduling and budgeting for the future, and she discovered she actually liked the feeling of not knowing what the future held.

At least, most of the future, anyway.

Jake was in meetings all day, either at Blackstone's or AdVance Corp, and when he finally came home, he sequestered himself in his office.

Despite her disappointment at being unable to publicly lay claim to him, to show him off in a burst of uncharacteristic womanly pride, the nights more than made up for it. They made love with a deep explosive passion, almost desperate in its intensity. Afterwards, in the dark, Jake revealed scraps of what his life had been like, how he'd come to scale the dizzying heights of the corporate world. She treasured those moments, storing them deep inside, knowing how much it took for this intensely private man to open up, even a little.

It meant hope, however meagre.

Many nights the words *I love you* teetered on the tip of her tongue, but she always ended up swallowing them. Yes, she desperately wanted to tell him how she felt. But she was also afraid. Afraid it would further add to what was already a complicated situation. That he wouldn't believe her and she'd drive him away.

Afraid she'd lose whatever little he offered her.

So instead she showed him. With her body, her hands, her lips, she showed him how desperately she loved him. It had to be enough for now.

And all too quickly, the night of the charity ball rolled around.

Jake was on the phone when Holly returned from her hair appointment. He caught a brief glimpse as she darted up the stairs, and when he'd followed her into the bedroom, found the ensuite door firmly closed, her "don't come in!" full of warning when he'd rapped on the door.

"I'll be in the kitchen," he replied through the door, glad he was already dressed.

He was staring out the kitchen window at a glittery cruise ship in the harbour when he sensed Holly behind him. Then he turned, and all brooding thoughts fizzled from his brain.

She was dressed in a white clingy creation, the vertical pleats emphasizing the gentle curves of her body. With her hair pulled high and back, curls cascading over her shoulders, she looked like some Egyptian goddess. The gauzy material draped across her breasts almost lovingly, and it was held up by small shoestring straps, leaving her arms bare. Beneath his unabashed staring, goose bumps spread over her skin.

"Is my dress OK?" She nervously tugged at the neckline, tweaking the fabric into place.

"You're more than OK."

Amazingly, after everything they'd done together, after every body part he'd teased, kissed and caressed, she blushed. He'd never get tired of seeing her blush.

Holly swallowed, suddenly breathless and more than a

little hot. It was as if he wanted to rip off her dress right then and there. And heaven help her, she wanted to let him.

Instead, she let her gaze roam over her husband-to-be. Jake had flaunted the black-tie requirement, instead choosing a black suit with a long dress coat, a pale green shirt and emerald cravat.

Under her careful study he grinned. "Acceptable?"

"Definitely. Me?"

"You're beautiful."

She swallowed, shifting her weight from one foot to the other. "Th-thank you."

He reached up, almost as if he was going to touch her cheek. She noticed a hesitation that revealed more than any words could.

Doubt swamped her. She'd spent the better part of the day with Kimberley and Jessica, first nailing down the last minute details, then being completely pampered with a half-day intensive makeover at Double Bay's exclusive Angsana Day Spa. Buoyed by the anticipation of the coming night, Kim had expressed her future vision for Blackstone's. Despite Holly's joy that Jake was included in those plans, Kim's predictions only served to exacerbate the glaring differences between her and the Blackstones, widening that chasm even more.

Now Jake's palm on her cheek seared her skin, branding her for ever. "I need to tell you something."

She leaned in to the touch, reveling in the gentle intimacy. "Yes?"

"Ric is going to announce our joint chairmanship tonight."

Holly eased away with a confused smile. "You and Ric will be running Blackstone's together?"

Jake nodded, absently running his thumb pad over the

curve of her cheek. "That's why I've been in all those meetings. He and Kim are building a house and want to start a family. He's had a shift in priorities."

"I see. That's...wonderful." It was. Really. The implication for Jake was huge. It meant he was a trusted family member of the highest standing. Yet all she could think of in the glow of his deep satisfaction was the growing canyon between them. This was just another small detail to glaringly highlight they were two completely different people.

She smiled brightly to cover up her burgeoning sadness then glanced at her watch. "We'd better go."

He nodded and placed a hand on the small of her back to lead her out the door. It was a warm brand of possession, one of such erotic simplicity that it made her insides ache. It felt as if every inch of her skin was aware and craved his touch, as if she couldn't get enough of it. As if she hungered for it.

Yet as she stared at him, all she could think of was how good he'd felt under her fingers, her lips. How much she wanted to lean over and kiss him.

How much she loved him. And how desperately she wanted to tell him, despite how it would irrevocably change everything.

They arrived at the ball amidst a press frenzy. The flash and pop of cameras lit up the red carpet like Oscar night, the air peppered with paparazzi calling out commands, eager for everyone's attention.

Holly stared out the car window and took a deep breath.

"Ready?" Jake murmured beside her.

She simply nodded.

As he exited the car an excited buzz went up from the assembled crowd.

Opening her passenger door, he extended his hand. The confident smile on his sensuous mouth set her nerves fluttering again, but for an entirely different reason. "Smile, Holly. We're engaged, getting married, and it's the best night of your life."

He'd never know she didn't have to fake it. She shoved all her niggling doubts firmly aside and smiled back at him. And then she firmly entwined her fingers in his, gathered up her skirts and stepped out into the waiting melee.

"Jake! Jake! A shot of you and your fiancée!"

"How does it feel to be finally getting married?"

"Have you set a date yet?"

"Holly! Who's going to be designing your wedding dress?"

The roar of the press, the flash of cameras came at her like a wave. She lifted a hand to shield her eyes, but Jake grabbed it and whispered, "Hand down. Smile as much as you can. Wave to the people. And pretend you're excited to be here."

"But I can't see!" she replied through a clenched smile.

"I know." His fingers tightened around hers as he waved back to the crowd and grinned. "It'll be over soon."

When he swept her into Blackstone's Grand Ballroom, the sudden noise drop made her ears ring. But in the next instant, she gasped.

The room was fit for a royal reception: dark purple velvet drapes edged with gold spanned the wide length. On top of white Grecian pillars sat huge golden decanters, pouring out black branches sprinkled with fairy lights. On the ceiling strings of tiny lights winked and sparkled, swooping low to meet the huge chandelier in the middle. Like an expensive diamond caught in the lights, the room shone—an apt backdrop for a Blackstone ball.

Yet after Jake's initial assessment, the room could have been knee-deep in desert sand for all the attention he gave it. Instead, he was mesmerised by Holly's satisfied smile on her dark pink lips, the kissy-mole creasing upwards.

Like a man suddenly wakened from a dream, he couldn't stop staring at her. Her profile, the way the shiny curls brushed the curve of her shoulders, his to touch if he so wished. And when she turned to look at him, pride glowing in her face, all at once a slow smile spread his mouth.

He could see the pulse beat in her throat, too great a temptation.

With a stubborn set to her jaw she looked right into his eyes and lifted her brow, a female imitation of his boardroom stare down.

I dare you.

He leaned in to kiss her, a kiss of such slow tenderness that something bloomed deep in his belly, something warm and protective and totally crazy. As he gently explored the shape of her mouth, his whole body began to vibrate.

"Aren't you going to introduce us, Jake?"

Holly started at Jake's soft oath, seeing the frustration tinge the edges of his expression, and smothered a chuckle.

Then she turned to the stunning blonde in a show-stopper strapless red dress, diamonds shimmering along the deep slit that rode high on one long tanned thigh. She needed no introduction to the woman labeled the Face of Blackstone Diamonds.

Briana Davenport.

"Briana." Jake kissed her lightly on the cheek, nonplussed when her date gave him a once-over, possessiveness clear in his blue eyes. "So you're the lucky guy who managed to land Briana."

"She picked me. And it looks like I'm not the only lucky one." He gave Holly a smile before shaking Jake's hand. "Jarrod Hammond. Congratulations on your engagement."

"Thanks. You're Matt Hammond's brother, right?"

As the men launched into a low discussion, Briana smiled at Holly and rolled her eyes. "Men. Remove them from the workplace and they still manage to talk about it. That's a gorgeous dress, by the way."

Holly returned Briana's genuine smile gratefully. "Thank you. I nearly tripped over the train three times."

Briana laughed. "Your first public outing is going well."

Holly grimaced. "I wish I was more like Kimberley, all grace and presence."

Both women's eyes landed on Kim, a vision of elegance in a black strapless floor-length creation, as she led the conversation in the circle of Blackstones.

"They all look fabulous, don't they?" Briana whispered. "Kind of regal. Almost perfect."

A perfect fit for Jake.

Her stomach dropped to her knees. *You knew what you were getting into. All the signs were there.*

According to Kim's vision, Jake would eventually take over Blackstone Diamonds and all that entailed. More money, more power, with a family who'd been denied to him for so long. Who did she think she was to demand his attention from all of that?

She closed her eyes for a brief second as pain ratcheted through her. How could she possibly let Jake go when their time was up? Yet she couldn't go back to her normal life as if nothing had happened.

She'd have to leave. Not just Blackstone, but possibly the

country. At least until the attention died down. There was no way she could remain here, feeling his presence in the halls, possibly even seeing him again.

Love wasn't in his plans, he'd made that perfectly clear. He needed her to see this deal through professionally, unemotionally.

She knew she was deathly scared, and in ignoring the deeper implications, she chose to protect her heart, to keep it intact so she could survive the rest of their time together. Self-preservation. That's what it was. And as much as she wanted to crawl into a tight ball and weep with the injustice of it all, she ignored it. Jake had been through enough, everyone had.

This was her gift to him.

As Holly watched, Ryan Blackstone said something to his wife and passed a gentle hand over her rounded belly. Jessica laughed, glowing in a shimmery silver halter-top gown.

An unexpected wave of longing smashed into Holly, freezing the smile on her face. Stunned, she blinked, glanced away…only to clash with Jake's all-seeing eyes.

She stiffened, desperately trying to dredge up a nonchalant smile to cover the raw emotion but failing abysmally. He wasn't just looking *at* her—he was looking deeper than that. His dark eyes glittered with something she couldn't quite fathom, something almost intimate and tender.

She held her breath.

"I don't believe it," Briana whispered. Holly followed Briana's shocked gaze and saw a tall man, resplendent in a black tux, standing apart from the crowd, flicking through the auction catalogue with a scowl on his handsome face.

"Matt Hammond," Jake said softly before taking Holly's hand in a firm grip and striding forward.

In a confused haze Holly kept up. Matt Hammond, Kimberley's ex-boss, Briana's brother-in-law, the widower of Marise. A man so committed to keeping the Blackstone-Hammond feud alive that he'd refused the ball invitation point blank when she'd called to confirm he'd actually received it. The man now in possession of four of the missing five Blackstone diamonds.

The closer they got, the more Holly felt trouble brewing. It wasn't anything overt, like Jake's commanding presence, more like a dark shroud of pain and betrayal covering the other man's impeccably dressed shoulders.

"Hammond," Jake said.

"Vance."

The two men shook hands and Holly was introduced, Matt acknowledging her with the barest of nods.

"What changed your mind about the invitation?" Jake said without preamble.

"Curiosity. I heard a rumor about some special announcement tonight." He flicked icy-cold eyes across the assembled throng that buzzed with the low throb of conversation and excitement. "And I wanted to see just how deeply the Blackstones had dug their claws into you."

Jake gave him a thin smile. "Wound-free, so far."

"Really." When Matt's gaze settled on Holly, she felt the shiver all the way up her spine. She bore the brunt of that deep, slow-burning anger with outward calm yet instinctively sought the warmth of Jake's hand. Without hesitation, he linked his fingers in hers.

Matt shifted his stance as a flash of something tightened his features. She'd thought Jake had a closet full of demons, but Matt Hammond had a thousand more.

"Quinn tells me you're looking for the last Blackstone Rose diamond," he said curtly.

Holly knew Matt Hammond had hit a nerve when she felt the tension vibrating through Jake's body. But she also knew his face would betray nothing. Still, she gave his rigid hand a reassuring squeeze, to let him know she was there if he needed her.

"That's right," Jake said.

"It's not yours to find."

"So?"

"So back off."

The air suddenly bristled palpably. Holly held her breath. For seconds—or was it minutes?—the two men faced each other off, not exactly adversarial yet worlds away from being friendly. Around them, people chattered, laughed, drank and ate, but the glittery event felt strangely muffled and dull around the edges of this small standoff.

Then, amazingly, Jake squeezed her fingers and in the next moment she felt his body relax.

"Only because you asked so nicely. And now, if you'll excuse us?"

Jake turned and, with a conspiratorial smile at Holly, drew her away.

"What was that about?" she whispered, pausing for the photographer before giving Jake her full attention.

"It's about knowing when to pick your moment, my sweet." He nodded over to the stage, to where Kimberley was adjusting the microphone. "The auction's about to begin."

"...and so, we have pleasure in introducing you to our eldest brother, James Hammond Blackstone."

There was a brief second of total stunned silence, a second in which Holly held her breath and tightened her grip on Jake's hand as they stood in the wings. But in the next instant, he smiled down at her, released her fingers and walked out onto the stage.

From behind the curtains, Holly dragged her eyes from his commanding figure to scan the crowd. The official photographers were going wild, snapping pictures of Jake, of the official handshake with a smiling Ric, of Jake accepting Kimberley's hug with practised ease. It was only when he came to Ryan that she saw him falter, a brief question in his face. Ryan nodded and instead of taking Jake's proffered hand, enveloped him in a hug.

Tears pricked behind her eyes, her heart swelling.

"Thank you all for your generous support tonight," a flushed Kimberley finally said over the din. "Please stay and finish the champagne. For those of you leaving, travel safely."

As they all left the stage, the noise level rose in one raucous wave, followed by flashing cameras exploding like tiny stars. Then the curtains abruptly fell, plunging the stage into muted normality.

When Jake spied Holly on the outskirts, fiddling with the tiny drop earrings in her lobe, his heart did a strange flip. She accepted everyone's congratulations with gracious aplomb, and when she looked up and spotted him, he echoed her heartfelt smile with his own, one of such unadulterated pleasure that he could see her flush from where he stood.

He devoured the space until she was in his arms. Slowly, deliberately, just because she was his and he could, he pulled her up against his length and kissed her. The truth of that kiss, the deep emotional connection they'd shared the past few weeks, floored him. Unmindful of where they were, he let his mouth leisurely roam over hers, pausing at the edge to lavish attention to that kissy-mole. Against him, he felt Holly stir, felt her warm sigh spill over his jaw, and just like that, he was ready.

"You need to stop," she muttered even as her neck tilted to give him better access.

He glanced across the room, to where the Blackstones were in animated discussion. "Can't stop."

Gently she placed her hands on his shoulders. "Must."

"Can't. Holly," he warned, stilling her. "Give me a minute. Unless you want everyone to know exactly how much I can't control myself."

As realisation heated Holly's cheeks, she felt the gentle rumble of Jake's chuckle, one full of intimate knowledge. And just like that, a deep, bone-jarring ache hit her. She wanted to spend the rest of her life with this man. She wanted to be the one to make him smile. To have his babies.

She blinked. What if that had already happened? They'd been using protection but nothing was foolproof. How could she justify leaving if Jake's child grew in her belly?

"You can turn around." His warm breath across her cheek jolted her back to the present. "We'll finish this later." His eyes held so much promise of pleasure to come that it made her forget every misgiving, every doubt.

At least, for tonight.

Twelve

Jake lingered in bed, unwilling to leave the warmth of Holly's soft, naked body. In truth, there was no place he'd rather be than here.

He reached for her, gently waking her with warm kisses. He loved the way she woke, all sleepy eyed and confused. As if she wasn't entirely sure she should be here, as if she'd emerged from a dream.

It was his dream—big, bold and erotic.

She blinked, twitching her nose as the delicious smell of hot coffee permeated the air.

"Morning," he muttered against her cheek.

She stretched, her curves moving in delightful torture against his growing arousal, and he felt her smile. "Is that coffee I smell?"

"Maybe." He nibbled her earlobe, grinning against her

neck as she shivered. In the next second, she leapt up and grabbed her robe, swishing it around her gloriously naked body with a laugh. "I'll be back."

He flopped back on the bed with a mock sigh. "Don't drink it all. And bring me a cup!" he called as she padded out the door.

An unfamiliar languorous warmth spread over his body, seeping into his bones.

He was…content. Happy.

Damn, he was ecstatic. For once, he felt like he belonged.

He'd been working hard these past few weeks, driven by the unfamiliar compulsion to convince the Blackstones of his commitment. He knew they were the kind of people who judged by deed, not words, so he'd personally ensured that Max Carlton was no longer a threat, that his mates on the board were quietly handed an ultimatum to leave or face criminal charges.

Instead of dark apprehension, he was surprised to feel relief. Relief it was all over, finally. He felt confident, almost optimistic, about the future. A future that hadn't felt so right until now. Until Holly.

He'd been missing something…something that began with a kiss and burnt bushfire hot when he and Holly made love. A flame he'd been determinedly ignoring in order to focus on the Blackstones.

The truth hit him like a speeding truck. What he'd been missing out on all those years while clawing his way to the top was family.

Yes, he'd had Quinn's family, but despite the glorious welcome they'd always given him, he'd always felt on the fringe, an outsider looking in. He'd been blessed with April.

She wasn't perfect or of his flesh and blood, but a generous, supporting woman all the same. One who loved him completely, who'd been prepared to do anything for him.

The power of a parent's love for a child was real; it was tangible. The kind of love Holly had for her mother and her father. The kind of love he wanted to share one day with his own child.

The object of his thoughts now stood in the doorway, fully dressed, a sheaf of papers in her hand.

"What, no coffee?" His teasing grin fell at the tight look on her face. His eyes went quickly to the papers. The prenup.

"When did you get these?" Her voice was light, almost calm.

"A few days ago."

"I need to sign them, yes?"

No. He sat up and nodded. With an odd, dignified composure, she made her way over to the bedside table, picked up a pen and signed with a flourish.

"Aren't you going to read it?"

She straightened. "I'm sure you've addressed every contingency, Jake."

He frowned as she walked over to the door. "I need to make sure the ballroom's been cleared plus Briana invited me to lunch later. I might not see you until tonight." She gave him a fleeting smile, devoid of warmth. Then she was gone.

What the hell had just happened?

He threw off the covers and grabbed the prenup. If she'd only just read it, she'd realise he wanted her for longer than a year. If fact, he was so confident about their deal that he'd actually made an allowance for babies resulting in the union.

It was all there, in black and white. Clause 22A paragraph C...

He paused as realisation suddenly hit, then groaned long and loud.

You fool.

With tears blurring her vision, Holly grabbed her handbag then slammed out the front door. Did she really think she could change this man with a bunch of kisses and a few nights of passionate lovemaking? He may have the Midas touch but no amount of gold could turn this marriage into a real one.

She stumbled and a strong hand yanked her up short. She whirled and came face-to-face with Jake, dark exasperation clouding his features.

"What are you—?"

"We need to talk."

"I'll be late." She pulled at his grip but her strength was no match for his. She had no choice but to follow him back into the apartment.

After he slammed the door behind them she backed away, crossing her arms. "What on earth are you doing?"

"I changed my mind. People do that sometimes."

But not you. Holly swallowed. "OK."

He took a breath, releasing it in a rush. "Is this about me co-chairing Blackstone's?"

Her chest contracted painfully. "No. This is a big thing for them, Jake," she said softly. "It means they trust you. You're truly a Blackstone now and all that entails."

"And what about you?"

"Is being a Blackstone something you want? Wait." He held up a hand when she opened her mouth. "For one second, forget about our deal—the money, the press. What do you really want, Holly?"

Fear rioted through her. She took a deep, shuddering breath meant to give her strength. Instead it robbed her of all rational thought.

"The party—those people…I'm just a country girl who still believes in love and you…" She waved her hand in his direction. "And now with the added weight and prestige of the Blackstone dynasty, where does that leave me?"

"You think we've made a mistake."

"Yes, I do." It was out there now, no going back. "I'll…I'll pay you back—"

He blinked, clearly taken aback. "Don't be ridiculous."

She forced herself to rise above the hurt and resentment. She'd pretended she could handle this maturely, but the truth was stark. She'd given her heart, and nothing short of his in return would have satisfied her. But he didn't offer it. Jake had been nothing but honest with her, laying down everything clearly and succinctly. She'd gone into this with open eyes and now she was the one wanting to change the status quo. He probably felt pressured and she couldn't blame him.

Her heart plummeted to her feet. "So it's just me you don't want."

Escape. Run. The fight or flight response snaked low in her belly and Holly shifted her weight, her calves aching from her hesitation. The air seemed to throb with life, the silence growing louder as he stared at her.

Then he smiled, shaking his head.

Her icy fear instantaneously melted into irritation. "You think this is funny?"

"I'm not laughing at you, Holly." He reached for her but she slapped him away, taking a step back for good measure. "And *I* thought I couldn't read what was right in front of me."

At her fierce glare, Jake's amusement dropped like a stone in water. A thousand unsaid words jumbled about in his head, none of them clever, none of them sane. He took a steadying breath to prepare himself. Still, he didn't know what to say.

The billionaire negotiator suddenly lost for words. Quinn would laugh himself silly at the irony.

Finally he spoke. From the heart. "Even when I left home, after I made my money, lost it, then gained it again, I always felt something was missing," he said slowly, picking his words with care. "Even with all the answers, there's…" He struggled with the admission before finally saying, "There's a hole. For years I thought it was guilt because I couldn't change the past no matter how much money I made." He allowed himself one moment of grief before shoving it away into the past, where it belonged. It was time to focus on the future.

"But now I know it's something else." He studied her keenly, trying to get handle on her thoughts. Her head was bowed, eyes focused on the floor, fingers threaded together in front. A lonely picture of defeat.

He nearly groaned. She unmanned him. He'd put those doubts in her stance with his stupid hesitation. Not any more.

"You asked where it left you. It's here, as my wife. Let me finish, Holly," he growled when her eyes snapped up and she opened her mouth. "Yes, this started out as purely a business deal. But right here, right now—" He broke off, took a shaky breath. "You touch me on a deep level, a level that includes both my head and my heart, in ways I never thought possible. Yes, my past was tough and shaped me into who I am today. But that's not who I am inside." He finally took her hand and placed it on his chest, and his throat clogged with emotion. "You saw that."

She closed her eyes briefly, as if his words pained her. But when she opened them, he was blown away by the love shining in those blue depths.

"I want you as my wife, my friend, my lover. I don't need the Blackstones to feel like I belong because I know I already do with you. I love you."

Holly couldn't breathe, couldn't move. The look in his eyes was so bare, so raw. So desperately needy that it made her want to cry.

She felt the telltale prick of tears behind her eyes. And when a sole tear slipped silently down her cheek, Jake reached out and caught it with one finger.

Slowly she smiled, joyfully throwing herself over the abyss. "I love you, too, Jake. Always. For ever."

They came together in a kiss, a tender kiss that gradually turned from gentle to aching in the blink of an eye.

Jake finally pulled back to search her face. "I want what Kim and Ryan have. A family, a future. A place I belong." His voice dipped lower, almost breaking. "Babies."

The love blazing from her eyes floored him. Humbled him. And filled him with so much joy that he felt like shouting it from the rooftops.

She was his. Now. For ever.

"Are you going to kiss me again, or what?"

He laughed and as he bent to accede to her demand, muttered, "I love you, Holly."

Her contentment seeped out against the gentle pressure of his lips, the promise of more, much more, to come.

Much later that day, Holly lay beside Jake, her fingers entwined in his in the cool silence. He'd finally unplugged the phone after the third call from his office and the second

rom first Kim, then Ryan. She sensed he'd detached
himself but knew she only had to touch him to bring him
back to her.

She knew his demons, knew them and still loved him for
it. She squeezed his hand, glanced up at her husband-to-be and
basked in the realisation that he was finally hers.

The gentle beep of Jake's mobile permeated the air but he
ignored it, instead saying, "Kim told me she'd talked to you
about Max."

"Mmm." Ridden with guilt, she'd finally confessed her in-
volvement last night. "You know what she said? 'If you'd
come to me, I'd have believed you.'" Holly shook her head.
Kim's blind acceptance of her innocence in the spy plot still
stunned her.

The rumble of Jake's laughter filled the bedroom. "Man, we
don't need anyone to complicate our lives. We do that all by our-
selves." He dodged Holly's nudge. "Kim also asked me to help
mend the rift between the Hammonds and the Blackstones."

Holly paused, recalling the look on Matt's face last night
following their revelation of Jake as James. Betrayal? Anger?
'It won't be easy. Matt Hammond is—" she searched for the
right word "—very committed to his bitterness."

"I live for a challenge."

She laughed. "Don't I know it."

He lifted himself up on one elbow, studying her intently.
"Are you ready for this— For the entire country to finally
know the complete details about the Blackstone Baby?"

"For as long as you want me, Jake Vance."

"Jake Blackstone," he corrected, before placing a gentle
kiss on her lips, a promise of things to come. "And that would
be for ever."

* * * * *

Don't miss the conclusion of
DIAMONDS DOWN UNDER
with JEALOUSY & A JEWELLED PROPOSITION
by Yvonne Lindsay, available in June
from Silhouette Desire.

THOROUGHBRED LEGACY
The stakes are high when it comes to love,
horse racing, family secrets
and broken promises.

A new exciting Harlequin continuity series coming soon!
Led by New York Times *bestselling author*
Elizabeth Bevarly
FLIRTING WITH TROUBLE

Here's a preview!

THE DOOR CLOSED behind them, throwing them into darkness and leaving them utterly alone. And the next thing Daniel knew, he heard himself saying, "Marnie, I'm sorry about the way things turned out in Del Mar."

She said nothing at first, only strode across the room and stared out the window beside him. Although he couldn't see her well in the darkness—he still hadn't switched on a light...but then, neither had she—he imagined her expression was a little preoccupied, a little anxious, a little confused.

Finally, very softly, she said, "Are you?"

He nodded, then, worried she wouldn't be able to see the gesture, added, "Yeah. I am. I should have said goodbye to you."

"Yes, you should have."

Actually, he thought, there were a lot of things he should have done in Del Mar. He'd had *a lot* riding on the Pacific Classic, and even more on his entry, Little Joe, but after meeting Marnie, the Pacific Classic had been the last thing on Daniel's mind. His loss at Del Mar had pretty much ended his career before it had even begun, and he'd had to start all over again, rebuilding from nothing.

He simply had not then and did not now have room in his

life for a woman as potent as Marnie Roberts. He was a horseman first and foremost. From the time he was a schoolboy, he'd known what he wanted to do with his life—be the best possible trainer he could be.

He had to make sure Marnie understood—and he understood, too—why things had ended the way they had eight years ago. He just wished he could find the words to do that. Hell, he wished he could find the *thoughts* to do that.

"You made me forget things, Marnie, things that I really needed to remember. And that scared the hell out of me. Little Joe should have won the Classic. He was by far the best horse entered in that race. But I didn't give him the attention he needed and deserved that week, because all I could think about was you. Hell, when I woke up that morning all I wanted to do was lie there and look at you, and then wake you up and make love to you again. If I hadn't left when I did—the way I did—I might still be lying there in that bed with you, thinking about nothing else."

"And would that be so terrible?" she asked.

"Of course not," he told her. "But that wasn't why I was in Del Mar," he repeated. "I was in Del Mar to win a race. That was my job. And my work was the most important thing to me."

She said nothing for a moment, only studied his face in the darkness as if looking for the answer to a very important question. Finally she asked, "And what's the most important thing to you now, Daniel?"

Wasn't the answer to that obvious? "My work," he answered automatically.

She nodded slowly. "Of course," she said softly. "That is, after all, what you do best."

Her comment, too, puzzled him. She made it sound as if being good at what he did was a bad thing.

She bit her lip thoughtfully, her eyes fixed on his, glimmering in the scant moonlight that was filtering through the window. And damned if Daniel didn't find himself wanting to pull her into his arms and kiss her. But as much as it might have felt as if no time had passed since Del Mar, there were eight years between now and then. And eight years was a long time in the best of circumstances. For Daniel and Marnie, it was virtually a lifetime.

So Daniel turned and started for the door, then halted. He couldn't just walk away and leave things as they were, unsettled. He'd done that eight years ago and regretted it.

"It *was* good to see you again, Marnie," he said softly. And since he was being honest, he added, "I hope we see each other again."

She didn't say anything in response, only stood silhouetted against the window with her arms wrapped around her in a way that made him wonder whether she was doing it because she was cold, or if she just needed something—someone— to hold on to. In either case, Daniel understood. There was an emptiness clinging to him that he suspected would be there for a long time.

* * * * *

THOROUGHBRED LEGACY
coming soon wherever books are sold!

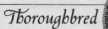

Thoroughbred *Legacy*

Launching in June 2008

A dramatic new 12-book continuity that embodies the American Dream.

Meet the Prestons, owners of Quest Stables, a successful horse-racing and breeding empire. But the lives, loves and reputations of this hardworking family are put at risk when a breeding scandal unfolds.

Flirting with Trouble

by New York Times **bestselling author**

ELIZABETH BEVARLY

Eight years ago, publicist Marnie Roberts spent seven days of bliss with Australian horse trainer Daniel Whittleson. But just as quickly, he disappeared. Now Marnie is heading to Australia to finally confront the man she's never been able to forget.

The stakes are high when it comes to love, horse racing, family secrets and broken promises.

A new exciting Harlequin continuity series coming soon!

www.eHarlequin.com

HT38984R

REQUEST YOUR FREE BOOKS!

2 FREE NOVELS
PLUS 2
FREE GIFTS!

Silhouette® Desire®

Passionate, Powerful, Provocative!

SDES08R

Royal Seductions

Michelle Celmer delivers a powerful miniseries in
Royal Seductions; where two brothers fight for the
crown and discover love. In *The King's Convenient Bride*,
the king discovers his marriage of convenience to the
woman he's been promised to wed is turning all too
real. The playboy prince proposes a mock engagement
to defuse rumors circulating about him and restore
order to the kingdom…until his pretend fiancée
becomes pregnant in *The Illegitimate Prince's Baby*.

Look for

THE KING'S CONVENIENT BRIDE

&

THE ILLEGITIMATE PRINCE'S BABY

BY MICHELLE CELMER

Available in June 2008 wherever you buy books.

Always Powerful, Passionate and Provocative.

COMING NEXT MONTH

#1873 JEALOUSY & A JEWELLED PROPOSITION—
Yvonne Lindsay
Diamonds Down Under
Determined to avenge his family's name, this billionaire sets out
to take over his biggest competition...and realizes his ex may be
the perfect weapon for revenge.

#1874 COLE'S RED-HOT PURSUIT—Brenda Jackson
After a night of passion, a wealthy sheriff will stop at nothing to
get the woman back into his bed. And he always gets what he wants.

#1875 SEDUCED BY THE ENEMY—Sara Orwig
Platinum Grooms
He has a score to settle with his biggest business rival. Seducing
his enemy's daughter proves to be the perfect way to have his
revenge.

#1876 THE KING'S CONVENIENT BRIDE—
Michelle Celmer
Royal Seductions
An arranged marriage turns all too real when the king falls for his
convenient wife. Don't miss the second book in the series, also
available this June!

#1877 THE ILLEGITIMATE PRINCE'S BABY—
Michelle Celmer
Royal Seductions
The playboy prince proposes a mock engagement...until his
pretend fiancée becomes pregnant! Don't miss the first book in
this series, also on sale this June!

#1878 RICH MAN'S FAKE FIANCÉE—Catherine Mann
The Landis Brothers
Caught in a web of tabloid lies, their only recourse is a fake
engagement. But the passion they feel for one another is all
too real.

SDCNM0508